I0646676

THE CHANGING WORLD OF TOMORROW

by

Ivan Golding

Grosvenor House
Publishing Limited

All rights reserved
Copyright © Ivan Golding, 2024

The right of Ivan Golding to be identified as the author of this
work has been asserted in accordance with Section 78
of the Copyright, Designs and Patents Act 1988

The book cover is copyright to Ivan Golding

This book is published by
Grosvenor House Publishing Ltd
Link House
140 The Broadway, Tolworth, Surrey, KT6 7HT.
www.grosvenorhousepublishing.co.uk

This book is sold subject to the conditions that it shall not, by way of
trade or otherwise, be lent, resold, hired out or otherwise circulated
without the author's or publisher's prior consent in any form of
binding or cover other than that in which it is published and
without a similar condition including this condition being
imposed on the subsequent purchaser.

This book is a work of fiction. Any resemblance to
people or events, past or present, is purely coincidental.

A CIP record for this book
is available from the British Library

ISBN 978-1-80381-867-2

My name is Tallulah Bell. And this is my pet duck. I named her Holly. She thinks that I am her mummy. And I love her very much but soon I will have to take her back to her real mummy. I hope that they too may overcome whatsoever tomorrow's world may bring. But God is the only one who has the answer to that.

Please notice that some of these characters mentioned in this book are partly fictional and have no relation to anyone bearing the same name in the real world.

THIS IS AN OBSERVATION ABOUT THE DEADLY UNSEEN KILLER COVID-19

I am a British-born child of West Indian descent. My name is Chanicia Golding. I just want to give these few lines of belated comfort to everyone across the world who has lost their loved ones to the unseen killer, Covid-19. It is important to acknowledge that Covid-19 not an ordinary flu as many people mistakenly believed. Countless children have been left without parents. And doctors and nurses have tragically lost their lives while trying to save others, leaving their own family behind. Now, to those who were unable to visit their loved ones before they passed away, I want you to know that someone empathizes and shares their grief.

My family and I are praying that God will give you the strength and comfort to carry on living with the hope that your loved ones are not altogether gone. 'They are like those who sleep in the morning. We are like grass that grows up. In the morning it flourishes; in the evening it is cut down, and withers away' (K.J.V. Psalm 90: v5 b).

In times of loss and sorrow, you may also take comfort, in the words of our Lord Jesus who said to a lady whose brother had died, 'I am the resurrection and the life; he that believeth in me, though he were dead, yet shall he live: And whosoever lived and believeth in me shall never die. Believeth thus this?' (K.J.V. Saint John 11:5).

CONTENTS

CHAPTER 1

COVID-19 HAD ARRIVED

When Owen Jarvis received news that his country was about to enter lockdown due to Covid-19, fear filled his eyes as he gazed towards the heavens. 'Oh, Lord my God,' he prayed, 'have mercy upon us.'

Covid-19 was about to add to his existing sorrows. He was already confined to his home, receiving treatment for cancer, he could only catch glimpses of the outside world through his windows. In this moment, he questioned God. 'Lord, will this pandemic mark the beginning of the end for my writing career?' Although it wasn't the first book he had written, it could potentially be his last. Then he begins pondering, 'Is there anyone who's able to tell whereabouts this deadly virus is coming from?' To this question he has no reply.

As the days wore on, three weeks before the country went into lockdown, one day a loud knock came on the door. Owen's wife, Deloris, went to answer the door and saw Simon Phillips, one of her husband's friends, standing there. 'Hello, Mrs Jarvis,' he spoke, 'can I see Owen for a minute?' he asked.

'Oh, no,' she said, 'I'm sorry, he isn't allowed any visitors because of Covid. But I can tell him that you've come to see him.' Then she shut the door behind her and went back inside, 'Owen, dear,' she called, 'your friend Simon Phillips was here to see you. I told him that you are not allowed any visitors. He said hi to you.'

However, while Simon Phillips was on his way home, he met a friend named Jeffrey Thomas. 'Hi, Simon,' Jeffrey spoke, 'guy, where are you going?' he asked.

He replied saying that he went to visit Owen Jarvis, but his wife, Deloris, said that he wasn't allowed any visitors. 'So I am on my way home.'

'Well,' Jeffrey spoke, 'could he not come to the door to see you?'

'He isn't allowed,' Simon replied, 'he has got many underlying health issues. This meant that Deloris would not allow him any visitors because of the risk of catching Covid.'

'I see,' Jeffery said, 'it now seems as if his days of socialising are over.'

'So, it seems,' Simon said. 'Why should one die trying to be brave?'

The years wore on very quickly. Owen spent three years under lockdown without having any visitors. One day he went outside and knelt down in the garden saying, 'Thank you, Lord God, for helping me to see the outside world again.' Then he got up from his knees and took a long, excited look around the area, and went back inside again. 'Deloris,' he called. He told her that he was back in in the house again. Then he went into the living room and slung himself down on the settee with joy.

A few minutes later his wife, Deloris, came in, dressed in a short, purple skirt and her white shirt tied around her waist. She came and kissed him on his chin, 'Darling,' she spoke, 'how do you feel going outside the first time after all those years you've spent inside?'

He looked at her with a smile. 'It was an experience, my dear,' he said, 'it was an experience.'

She took hold of his hand, saying, 'You'll have to keep going outside until you have got used to going out again. Can I ask you a question?' she added.

'Of course,' he said. 'Go ahead.'

'Can you remember telling me some time ago that you saw a rubber tyre full of gold buried beside a road in Harehills, West Yorkshire?"

'Yes,' he replies excitedly. 'There was enough gold in that tyre to support a country for a whole year!'

She replied, 'Can you remember the road and the place where you saw the tyre?'

'Yes,' he said, 'clear as a crystal, but that was in 1977. Now it is 2023. Even if the gold were still there nobody would be allowed to dig up the road.'

She thought about it for a moment then said, 'I don't think for a moment that anybody in Harehills could have had so much gold?'

Owen looked at her and said, 'Deloris, before the past World War it could be that many rich people were resident in Harehills. Someone must have buried their gold there for safekeeping and got killed in the war, and hadn't any family, so the gold had been left behind.'

'Well,' she spoke, 'if they were allowed to dig up the road then, why are they not allowed to dig it up now?'

Owen replied, 'The person might have buried it there before the road was made.' He said that he hadn't any proof.

The reality was that he had seen the buried gold one day while he found himself driving along the Harehills road toward the city. Just before he came to the corner where the dead rested on the left and there was a hospital on the right, he turned a sharp left up a side road that led toward Harehills Lane. As soon as he came up to a slip road that came from Harehills road and formed a V, his minibus began skidding until it made a hole in the road. That's when he saw the rubber tyre full of gold and, being excited at the thought of becoming rich, he woke up out of his sleep.

'Well,' she spoke, with a smile on her beautiful face, 'I see. You've found your riches and left it there for somebody else to inherit'.

Owen couldn't deny that was the truth. He didn't even go back there and had a look.

CHAPTER 2

A RIDDLE

Three months after Owen Jarvis got used to the outside world again, one morning his wife, Deloris, got up for work. Before she left the house, she called her husband, Owen, saying that she almost forgot to let him know that a decorator would be coming to the house in the morning.

'Decorator?' He repeated his concern about the cost.

'Don't you worry,' she said, 'I had all the money I needed to pay the workers.'

He breathed out a "wow" and gave her a clap. Then he said within himself, *I hope they don't disturb our neighbours.*

Next morning, bright and early, the decorator came, just in the nick of time. They were just about to go off to work. She went immediately to the door with a big smile on her face. But after she heard the overall cost of the painters, she hung her head. Owen decided to do the work himself.

Two weeks later, one morning Owen got out of bed early and started to work. His wife noticed that he had been working for a long time without having a break. She fetched him a cup of coffee. Just as he was about to take a sip, one of their friendly neighbours, who was passing, saw him painting the outside window. 'Hello, Owen,' he uttered, 'I didn't know that you're a painter!'

'There's always a first time,' he replied.

Then the stranger came a little closer toward the house, speaking quietly. 'Owen, have you heard what those poor people in Ukraine are suffering?'

'Yes,' he said, 'those soldiers are heartless people. They are killing both woman and children just because they wanted to live the freedom of a democratic life.'

Then the stranger spoke up again. 'Jarvis, may I tell you a story in a riddle?'

'Oh, yes,' he said. 'Go ahead.' Deloris stood still with a smile waiting to hear what the riddle was about.

The stranger began by saying, 'Once upon a time there lived a farmer that kept honeybees. His bees were harmless until a swarm of killer bees came to take over their hives by frost. Then one day the farmer went to feed his bees and got stung. He immediately found out that killer bees were trying take over the hive. He searches until he finds the killer bees' queen. He says to her, "You will not make any more of your killer bees' eggs in my hives." Upon saying this, he took the killer bees' queen out. And as soon as the rest of the killer bees heard that their queen had been taken out, they all surrendered themselves to the former bees and they live in peace ever after.'

Deloris gave the stranger a clap and her husband said, 'Wow.'

Then Deloris looked at the stranger and said, 'Do you know the meaning of the riddle you've just told us?'

'Of course,' he said. 'It is just logic that if a person gave out a riddle, they would have known the meaning of it.'

She spoke again with a smile, saying, 'We don't know the meaning of the riddle, so can you tell us what it meant?'

Before the stranger replied, Owen looked and saw some of his grandchildren coming to visit them. Leona first coming through the gate, followed by Aaliyah and her younger sister, Tallulah. 'Hi, Grandad,' they uttered. Then they went and greeted their grandmother who was standing at the door.

Deloris gives them a hug and kiss, then says goodbye to the stranger. She went inside the house with the children. Now that Deloris and had gone. The stranger said goodbye to Owen and went on his way.

After the stranger had gone, Owen stopped working, put away his brushes and paint and went inside the house to see his grandchildren.

CHAPTER 3

A LOW-FLYING AEROPLANE

While they were talking, one of the children said, 'Grandad, can we go outside in the garden?' It was sunny and bright out there, being the summer month of July. Owen had a change of clothes and went outside with the children. As soon as the children took a seat outside, they saw an aeroplane flying low with its wheels down as it was about to land.

The children there all got excited looking at the aeroplane whilst pointing fingers at it.

The older one said to the others, 'Why the excitement, haven't any of you seen an aeroplane landing before?'

'Yes,' one answered, 'but this one is flying ever so low and there isn't an airport to be seen.'

'There is an airport of course' said Grandad. 'But it is about eight miles away from here.' Then he told the children that when his sons and daughter, their parents, were about their age, he and his wife used to take them to the airport just to look at aeroplanes landing and taking off again. It's just that these days they don't allow onlookers at airports anymore. But it wasn't so in the '70s. People were free to visit airports and had cups of tea or coffee while they looked at aeroplanes landing and lifting off again.

As soon as he said this, one of his grandchildren said, 'Grandad, can you tell us a story.'

'Of course,' he said, 'what should the story be about?'

She said, 'Tell us a story about Owen Jarvis's childhood days in the West Indies.'

He looks at her and said, 'That's a jolly good idea. Why didn't I think of that before?'

In his heart he would love nothing better than to tell the children a story that was based on Owen Jarvis's youthful days growing up in the West Indies. But on the other hand, the children might not stay with him long enough to hear the story to the end because their parents would be coming shortly to take them home. So, he made them a promise that he'd write the story and then they could read it whenever they wished.

CHAPTER 4

THE BELATED BIRTHDAYS

Before the children went home with their parents, one of them looking at her mother said, 'Mum within three weeks' time it will be your father's birthday. You've told me how excited he was on his last birthday, and I can't wait to see the shine on his face this time.'

'Yes,' her mother said. 'We will give him a birthday that he has never had before.'

Three weeks later was her dad's birthday. She and her family went early, to be her dad's first guests. But when they got there some of the other families were there before them. Owen Jarvis's sons and daughters and their children and other guests gave Owen a birthday celebration he would

never forget. Then at the end of the day Owen and his family went outside and had his photograph taken. But he had forgotten to tell his writer about the story so he apologised to the children and made them new promise.

Two weeks after her grandad's birthday, Leona went back to see him and reminded him to get the story started as promised. As soon as he saw Leona come through the gate, he went to meet her, saying, 'Don't you worry, my beauty, I am going to get it started straight away.' Then he took up the telephone and began to think of young Owen Jarvis's days in the West Indies. She said goodbye to her grandad and told him that she would come back one day soon and away she went.

CHAPTER 5

THE SPECKLED BIRDS

Owen Jarvis was born in the Parish of Manchester in Jamaica. His mother's name was Megan and his father's, Uriah. Megan brought up her children at two different homes. Sometimes she and her children would be spending time at her parents' home in Clarendon. At other times, she would be with her husband and children at her home in the Parish of Manchester.

Owen Jarvis and his brothers and sisters love to stay at their grandparents' home in Clarendon. Young Owen was happier there because at his parents' home in Manchester there was a large cotton tree at the bottom of the garden. The cotton tree was very large and everyone thought that it was very selfish. Because of all the other trees, it lived alone at the bottom of the garden in the middle of the valley, and it wouldn't allow anybody to climb up it made sure that they didn't by making itself prickly. From the root of the tree to the very top, the branches were covered with thorns.

Then, to Owen's horror, one day while he was on his way to school, passing the cotton tree, he looked and saw a

large, speckled bird upon the panicle branch looking down to towards the ground. As soon as the bird saw him it flew off into the sky, showing the freedom of flying about in the air. The bird flew high over the hills and low over the valley and then it came to rest at the top of the cotton tree. It stayed there just for a while and then flew down to the ground not far from where Owen Jarvis was standing. And immediately a miracle happens that caused Owen's hairs to stand on end. The speckled bird now became a beautiful young girl of about his age. She was dressed in the same colour clothes as that of the speckled bird's feathers. Young Owen Jarvis was scared out of his wits. He stood like a mute child looking at the girl. As soon as he regained his senses, he set off to run. The young lady saw him running away.

'Please don't run,' she said, 'I just want to be your friend.' Owen didn't stop. She shouted out again, 'Please don't tell your friend that you've seen me!' Owen didn't reply he just kept running until he caught up with his school friends. They went on to school, but he didn't say a word to them about the mysterious lady bird that he had saw.

After school, as soon as he came home, he went alone to the bottom of the garden, so that he might not disturb the lady bird. He went on timidly until he reached the nearest tree to the cotton tree. Then he tiptoed a little closer until he has a clear view of the cotton tree. With trembling legs, he took a timid look at the tree from the root up to the very top branches, but he didn't see the speckled bird that evening, so he went back home with a thought in his heart.

Three months later, while he was on school half term, he promises to meet friends at a place known as beauty spot. But his parents wouldn't have allowed him to go there on his own. But he moaned and moaned until Lewis, his older brother, decided to go with him.

The beauty spot was at the lower part of a high mountain beside the Caribbean Sea, many miles away from where he lived. Children often went there to looked at large ships sailing the deep seas and the local fishermen in their rowing boats heading for home. They would wave hands and shout out hello to the passengers in ships. Just for fun, knowing that they will neither see nor hear them. The beauty spot was a lovely place with lots of places to view from there. Young people and adults usually went there to take refuge from the strong heat of the day. There were plenty of fresh green grasses alongside the mountain. And in the strong heat of the day, the cool wind blowing from the sea flickered the grasses, so they looked like a rippling stream of water flowing down the hill.

However, the day had grown much colder now. Owen and his school friends and his brother went and stood at the lower part of the mountain. There was clear view across the sea. They looked as far as their eyes could see until the sea became a border with the sky. It was a calm, clear day. The light of the sun was dazzling upon the waters. Owen looked into the sea and called his brother in excitement. 'Lewis, please, come and take a look at this!'

'Isn't it gorgeous,' he said.

'It's unforgettable,' agreed the others.

Then they moved on to another part of the mountain where thousands of butterflies were hovering in trees of multi-coloured blossoms and sea birds flew over the water. They would take their catch from the water and fly to the mountain to dine in the trees. Then suddenly they saw the shadow of a large bird flying over the mountain going toward the sea. Owen saw it and his heart leapt. He thought that was the shadow of the speckled bird that lived in the cotton tree at the bottom of his parents' garden now come to haunt him by the sea. But when it came into view, he breathed out a sigh of relief; it was one of those red hawks, which were birds' greatest enemy. As soon as the sea birds saw the shadow of the hawk's outstretched wings, they all flew away and hid themselves within the rocks. The hungry hawk flew low over the water. It was looking here and there into the sea, but the fishes might have hidden themselves, so the hawk set off again and away it went.

CHAPTER 6

THE FARM WORKERS

After the hawk had gone, Owen and his brother and friends returned to their home. Two days later, Owen was in the garden pulling some grasses from among the young vegetable. He looked and saw some that some fruit trees around the garden were ready for harvesting.

In those days, when Owen was a child, the work at his parents' home seemed to be endless. His parents were very strict in their traditions. Most of the farm work had to be done on a Friday. Saturday was their Sabbath. So, they gave all the children a job to do. Owen's job was to take home the animals on Fridays; as soon as he came home from school, take them to a plot of land, and feed them there. And when that plot had been trampled and the rain came upon it, it yielded a rich fertiliser that cost nothing.

Pigs and hens were free to go about in the garden but the hens with chicks needed special attention or else their young ones would be taken by hungry mongooses or red hawks.

Most people who raised chickens would have had specially trained dogs to protect their hens. In the West Indies, the red hawks and ravens are very large birds, and the red hawks are the most aggressive ones. They would fly down quickly to snatch a young chicken, and despite the mother hen trying her best to fight them off, the hawks were always the winner. They would take their catch quickly and make a fast escape before the dogs got hold of them. But sometime times they left an injured hen behind.

Mongooses were less fortunate. Sometimes they got caught by dogs, or escaped by reaching their hole or climbing up into a tree. Creatures such as mongooses fed on birds and young chickens and crabs. Sometimes the crabs would put up a challenge against them and left a claw mark on them. They became an easy catch for the dogs. In Eastern Manchester, dogs and mongooses are the worst of enemies. The mongooses had their own technique of getting away from dogs. They would take their catch quickly and make a fast escape into a small hole between rocks that were too small for the dog.

As the years wore on, children got older. Owen Jarvis was much older now. While he was at home alone one day, he began to imagine being in a perfect world, where none of the aggressive people dwelt. The senior citizens there were loved and were never mugged. In that world nobody was treated indifferently because of their age or their disability or creed. Obviously, who can tell what their tomorrow is going to be like? The young will get old someday, not to be attacked and be mugged but to be loved and cared for.

Two weeks later, Albert Clarence, one of Owen's friends, came to visit him at home. They went for a walk about the garden and sat beneath a fruit tree which was laden with green and ripe fruits. Albert looked around the area. 'Owen,' he spoke, 'I was just thinking about the Parish of Manchester and why people who come from overseas call it "land of paradise"?'

'That's right,' said Owen. 'Manchester is a very beautiful place. The trees are evergreen, summer or winter they remain the same. In the Parish of Manchester most of the native people live on their own cultivated land. They have many fruit trees. And at certain times of the year, some of them would be ready for harvesting. They would have looked like flowers on the trees as they hang towards the ground.'

CHAPTER 7

JAMAICA'S COUNTRYSIDE

One day, Owen Jarvis and his mum, Megan, were in garden. Ralph, one of Owen's friends, came to visit him. Owen left his mum in the garden. He and Ralph went for a walk. They climbed up the slope of a hill near the garden. From there, there were clear views of the valley below, which was full of young trees. Ralph looked over the valley towards a beautiful landscape a distance away.

He looked at Owen and said, 'The Parish of Manchester is indeed a very beautiful place to live.'

'Yes,' Owen said. 'All this island needs is people with plenty of money to build up the area into holiday resorts. Having lots of houses and hotels.'

The Parish of Manchester does produce many kinds of fruits and food and vegetables through the year. The mystery of the island was that, however hard it might rain, as soon as the rain stopped the ground would dry up quickly. The earth

never went as soggy as the other part of the island did. In the Parish of Manchester there were certain fruits that could not be exported to far-off countries because they were too fragile. Fruits such as the naseberry, avocado pears, mangoes and bananas easily ripen. If they were to be exported, they must be harvested at a very early stage. The fruit that the guy is pointing to is known as sweetsop. As soon as the skin between the pegs gets yellow, they are ready for harvesting. This one is already ripe and ready to be eaten. The pegs inside are white like milk and very delicious; if you tasted it, you would love it.

CHAPTER 8

THE GUARD DOG

The days of the weeks and the months of the years had worn on very quickly. One weekend, Owen Jarvis and his friend, Josh Winter, went for a walk at the seaside. On their return, they heard the sad news that one of Owen's parents' guard dogs had gone missing. Owen's immediate thought was that the dog might have chased after a mongoose and got itself trapped in a small hole and was unable to get out. Having all these thoughts, he and his friend and his brother, Lewis, went to search a piece of woodland not far from their home. As they walked from stage to stage, they called the dog, by its name, Bigley, but they didn't hear a sound from it. So, they returned home and planned to start a new search first thing in the morning.

Next morning, bright and early, Owen Jarvis woke up, sprang out of bed and went outside in a rush to see if the dog had returned, but it had not. So, two groups of people went out to search again. They planned to meet up at a place called the spring, which was not far from the Caribbean Sea. Owen Jarvis and his group of fellows went to search at the lower part of the mountain where they had often taken the dogs for a walk. The other groups of fellows went to search the woodland near the spring. On their way through the woodland, they came upon many different kinds of fruit trees, some of which were known as thirst-quenchers. They looked like grapes, but they were filled with nice, cool, sweet liquid.

By this time, the gangs had been searching for many hours but had neither seen nor heard the dog. The day had grown much older now. The sun was high in the sky. Owen Jarvis and his group of fellows now came to the spring. There the others were waiting for them. One of the guys saw them coming to the spring. 'Owen,' he called, 'have you found the dog?'

'Oh, no,' he mumbles in a sad voice.

'Neither have we,' they said.

They had all met at the spring now. The sun was scorching hot. The boys were tempted to go for a swim in the river. They should have thanked their lucky stars. Three ladies who were passing saw them. 'Guys,' one lady calls, 'do not go into the water.'

'Why not?' asked one of the guys, in a rude tone of voice.

She said, 'There's an alligator in the river.'

The boys were dumbstruck! There all went silent for a moment. Then one of them looked at the ladies and in a fearful tone of voice he said, 'Lady, are you kidding us?'

'Oh no,' she said. 'My friend and I saw it this morning on our way to the beach. Didn't we?' she asked her friend.

She said, 'Yes.'

Then the guys apologised to the ladies for being rude to them. They had thought that the ladies were giving them a telling off, as they were not allowed to swim in the river.

As soon as the ladies had gone, one of the guys went to the river and had a look into the water. But he didn't see the alligator. He shouted, 'Thank you, ladies!' But by this time, the ladies had gone out of sight.

CHAPTER 9

IT'S LIKE A LOG

Now they had heard of the alligator in the water they couldn't help feeling excited. One of them timidly crept up to the side of the river and took a look into the water. He saw what looked like a piece of log floating far off downstream toward him. 'That's the alligator,' one guy yelled out, frightened. The others went to the side of the river just in time to see the alligator pop its head above the water.

'It's a huge beast,' said one.

'Let us stone it,' says the other. Then they started throwing stones in the water at the alligator, while the others laughed.

Owen Jarvis took a look at the time. The day had almost far spent. The sun was now going down beyond the sea. Shadows of darkness were creeping up slowly into the woodland. 'Guys,' Owen calls to the others, 'it's time for us to go home.' As they delayed, he shouted out again. 'Guys, let us be on our way.' It was getting dark and there wasn't any light in the woodland. Then they were on their way, walking along a small dirt road through a field.

'Owen,' one guy calls, 'I was just thinking...'

'About what?'

'That your dog might have been eaten by the alligator.'

Owen turned sharply to look at him, saying, 'Don't you ever say that to me again.'

Even though he knew perfectly well in his heart that his friend might be right, he didn't want to be thinking that way. So, the guy apologised, saying, 'Owen I am truly sorry, I shouldn't have spoken that way.'

'It's OK, it's OK.'

CHAPTER 10

THEY KEPT SEARCHING

At nightfall, Owen Jarvis and one of his older brothers went out again to search the woodland. They called the dog by name, then stopped to listen but they couldn't hear a sound. So, they returned home with a hope that the dog might return next day. But sadly, it didn't return then, either.

In those days when Owen Jarvis was a boy living at home with his parents, there wasn't any electric light in the villages. The streets were always dark at night. They didn't have any refrigerators or washing machines in the house. The toilet was outside the house. The nearest shower rooms were a distance away from the village. Ladies of home would take their washing to the tubs. And their food and vegetables would be taken straight from the garden. By doing so they had fresh food and fresh vegetables daily if they so desired. The fishermen in the village would do likewise. They would have got out of bed early in the morning and went off to sea in their rowing boat to fish. The people who made their living by selling fresh fish to the people in the villages would be on the beach waiting until the fishermen returned from the sea. The local butchers in the village would do likewise. They would go around the villages and take orders from the villagers and serve them fresh beef or mutton according to what they required.

In those days, when Owen Jarvis was a child at home with his parents in the Parish of Manchester, Jamaica, each child had their own duty to perform. Owen's duty was to bring home the animals in the evening after school and feed them at a special plot of ground. He used to have lots of fun bringing the animal's home. He didn't have any trouble bringing them home. There was a leader among the flock that the others followed so Owen had no problem. There weren't modern aids to farming in those days. Fertilizer was expensive. The small farmers such as Owen's parents couldn't afford it, so they used the age-old way to enrich their land with the animals.

CHAPTER 11

PLAYING ON THE BEACH

As soon as Owen Jarvis and his friends came home from school, they would take up their cricket bats and ball to play cricket. One afternoon, as soon as they came home and were about to run off to play, Owen and his friend, Josh, were told that they were not allowed to go to the beach to play at that time of the evening. Owen and Josh were part of the team. But when they came home from school their parents said that it was too late for them to go to the beach which was about 20 miles away from home. Owen would have to take the animals home first. He begged and begged but his parents told him that he could not go. 'Mum,' he called, 'my friends and I are a part of a team.' However, later that evening, the others returned, saying that the match had to be cancelled because there wasn't enough daylight left for them to play.

Six months later some of the produce in Owen Jarvis's parents' garden was ready for harvesting. The pimentos trees would bear fruit only once a year and would have to be harvested as soon as they were ready. Owen Jarvis and some of his friends had now reached their intermediate age. It was now time for them to help in reaping and sowing. But, as children, all they wanted to do was hang out with some of the older boys and girls in the village.

In two weeks' time it would be the national holiday. Most of the young people in the villages were preparing to go to the festival. Their famous DJs would be there. This would be Owen Jarvis's first visit to a festival. It was also his first social day out with his older friends. He was so excited and he couldn't wait to see the day.

On the day of the festival, he couldn't believe his eyes. There were thousands of young boys and girls doing the twist again. The kind of dancing that he hadn't seen before. The music at the festival was so loud it could be heard from several miles away. The sun was very hot and those in the hall dancing were sweating; body and faces were wet. Most people were outside dancing on the grass in the common. Young Owen Jarvis was ever so excited, he looked around and breathed out with a "wow". He had never seen so many young people at any one place before. Most of the young ladies were in their summer dresses. When he went into the hall where the music was it was like walking into a garden full of sweet-smelling flowers. There was more excitement to be seen. There was a dancing contest going on in the next hall which was hot as hell. Owen had never seen people doing the latest dancing before.

CHAPTER 12

THE REMOTE VILLAGE

Then, to Owen's disappointment, at the end of the day and when it had become night, his friends were going back to the festival, but he wasn't allowed to go with them, no matter how hard he might cry. Just because it was at night-time. In those days, some parents did not allow children at a certain age to have a night life. They had also brought up their children to pay respect to the older generation and help them whenever they are in need of help. By doing so, children learnt to love and care for their senior citizens.

Mr Cedric was one of the elderly people living in the remote part of the village. They had no electric lights so they would use lamps in their houses. Some of them used the age-old method to find their way home at night: they laid stones on both sides of the garden path that led to their houses and painted them white. Then, on moonless nights, they were able to find their way to their houses much more easily. Most of the elderly people living in the remote part of the village found it very difficult to get around at night, especially on a moonless night. Their garden paths had been crowded with fruit trees that make the pathway dark, especially at night. Jarvis and other children in the village made it their duty to go and visit old-age pensioners and do little jobs for them so that they might not feel altogether cut off from the community. Some of the older people in the village loved to give children gifts. In those days, fruits were the most favourite of gifts. Old Cedric was one of the children's favourite friends. He was kind to everybody, especially to children.

Despite Mr Cedric being one of Jarvis's nearest neighbours, his many acres of land kept them far apart.

One evening after school, Jarvis went to bed at his usual time. As soon as he rested his head upon his pillows he began to doze and the night now became as day. He now found himself with three of his friends, Justin Thomas, Robert Wills and George Sampson. They were on their way to visit some of the older people living in the difficult part of a remote village. So they decided to visit Mr Cedric first. They went to his house, knock-knock-knocked at his door, but had no reply. Mr Cedric had always been an active old man; he could have been anywhere on his many acres of plantations. Especially as it was at a time when some of his fruits were ready for harvesting. Because he was an old person, the children decided to go and search for him. This could be very difficult because he could be anywhere. He had many acres of highly cultivated land. As soon as the children walked some way, they began to shout out his name with all the loudness of their voices. 'Mr Cedric!' they called once, twice, but had no response.

By this time the day had grown much older. The children had cause for concern, not knowing whether the old gentleman was alive or not. However, after they had called and searched and had no answer, they decided to go back home and let their parents know that they hadn't seen old Cedric. Mr Cedric was a very good friend of everybody in the village. They all knew that he was a very kind person. Whenever you bumped into him, he would be wearing a pleasant smile. He was someone who would help others the best he could. Jarvis and his friends were now on their way, running and walking for home. At length they came upon the main road that separated Mr Cedric's land from his neighbours. At this point the boys split up and went their different ways home. From the main road to Jarvis's parents' home, it was an uphill journey. He ran until he reached so far up the hill he had to stop to catch a breath. Then he looked back over the valley and caught sight of Mr Cedric in his place.

CHAPTER 13

ECHOES OVER THE VALLEY

Owen Jarvis was glad that he had seen Mr Cedric alive. He shouted out with all the loudness of his voice, 'Hello, Mr Cedric!' Then he waved his hand, but Mr Cedric didn't react to him as if he didn't want to communicate with anybody that day. *What is wrong with Mr Cedric today?* he asked himself. Mr Cedric had never acted in such a way before, especially towards children. He seemed somewhat desperate. He was a worried-looking man.

Then, while Owen was standing there, he saw two men who looked like police officers giving Mr Cedric chase. Then they caught him. They lifted him up off his feet, turned him upside down and shook him until all the contents in his pockets fell to the ground. Jarvis wanted them to know that he was watching them. He shouted out, saying, 'Leave Mr Cedric alone, he's a good person. He never harms anyone.' All Owen Jarvis heard was the echoes of his own voice over the valley repeating the same thing back to him. Next morning, when Owen Jarvis woke up out of his sleep, he was dumbfounded that he was only dreaming.

As the day grew older, he heard that Mr Cedric had been arrested. He was lost for words to explain the sorrow that was in his heart for his old friend.

CHAPTER 14

COUNTRY BOYS

As the years wore on, one day Owen Jarvis and a friend went to shop in Kingston market and Owen was very angry. Whenever he and his friend came up some of those boys who live in a big city such as Kingston they would made a mock of them, calling them "country boys". Jarvis and his friends used to get very angry with them until they realized that it was much healthier for the people who lived in the country as those who lived in the city suffered from the increases in greenhouse gas pollution.

Jamaican countryside in those days was a beautiful place to live. There were many trees of multi-coloured blossoms. Some of the fruit trees were always laden with green and ripe fruits. The sweet-scented blossom of some trees would blend with the fresh air from the sea and everybody who took a sniff would breathe out with a "wow". There were many beautiful landscapes with the view of waterfalls in the distance. The village where Owen Jarvis was born and raised wasn't far from the Caribbean Sea. He and his brothers and friends use to have lots of fun playing on the beaches. Until they got hungry when they would return home to eat Mummy's tasty cooked food.

Owen Jarvis used to love going to school until one school day a boy in his class made him feel humiliated. All because he couldn't read as fast as the other children. One boy in the class usually looked at him and then glanced at his friends and they had a laugh. If there was help for dyslexic children in those days, perhaps Owen Jarvis's parents would've known of it. Owen would try to avoid going to school on a reading day because the guys might embarrass him again. And whenever he was provoked his blood pressure got higher than it should. Sometimes he was on the edge of having an explosion. Doctors couldn't understand why this young man's blood pressure kept on going so high after all the medication he had taken.

Had doctors known the cause of it, perhaps they would have given him some other treatments that might stop his pressure rising.

CHAPTER 15

TIME FOR A CUPPA

Many years had passed and now Owen Jarvis became a family man living in England with his family. One afternoon, while he was at home, he went outside the house and sat alone in the garden. His thoughts went back to his boyhood living at home in the West Indies with his parents. Then his wife, Deloris, came and sat beside him. 'Darling,' she spoke, 'I am going to make a cup of tea, would you like one?'

'Of course,' he said.

She got up, took a few steps forward and then turned sharply. She looked at Owen, saying, 'I have a bone to pick with you.'

'About what, dear?' he asked.

She looked at him again and changed her mind, saying, 'I'll tell you about it later.' Then she went back inside and into the kitchen.

After she had gone, Owen wondered to himself, *why has she changed her mind?*

However, about five minutes later she returned with two cups of tea and biscuits in a saucer. After they have eaten and drunk, she took Owen by his hand, saying, 'Darling, I was just thinking, why didn't my parents give me a better name than this I have?'

'Your name is beautiful,' Owen said. 'I love your name. It sounds like a quiet flowing stream of water flowing in my ears.'

'Is that so?' she asked, smiling.

'Yes!' Owen said. 'Very much so.'

She turned and looked at him, saying, 'I've heard that in your intermediate age, girls were developing a crush on you?'

'Well,' he gasped, 'you are very jealous, aren't you?'

'Oh no,' she said, 'I was just thinking that age does spoil beautiful figures. Don't you think so, darling?' Then they hugged each other and had a laugh. Then she took the cups and saucers back to the kitchen.

About half an hour later, Aaliyah, one of their granddaughters, came to visit them, riding on a horse. Owen shouted to his wife, Deloris, 'Our granddaughter, Aaliyah, is here to see us.'

'Hello, Gramma,' she called, 'I am going for a ride with my friends, I just stopped to say hello.' Before she left, she said, 'Grandad, can I asks you a question?'

'Of course, dear,' he said. 'Fire away.'

'When Owen Jarvis was a child of about 12 years old, what was the most exciting things that children of that age would most love to have? I love to have horses.'

'Well,' Owen replied, 'this is going to be a long story and you are getting late. So I'll put that question and answer into a story book and then you can read it whenever you like!' She agreed and off she went.

After she had gone, Owen Jarvis began to dream up his youth days. In those days, when he was a boy of about 12 years, every child his age would have most loved to have a bicycle. That was one of the most important gifts that parents

could give their child at the time. Having a bicycle in those days would be like a young man having a sports car in these days. Children like to have things that move fast. A bicycle was one of their favourite choices. They used it to race against each other. When Owen finally reached 12 years old, he got his first bicycle. He used to clean it every day and put plenty of lights on it. At night his bicycle was like a Christmas tree running on the road. One evening after school, Owen Jarvis and his friend, Josh Ward, went out for a ride in the district. Not far from home they came upon two guys who were a little older than they were. 'Hi, guys,' uttered one.

'Where are you going?' asked the other.

Josh replied, 'We are going for a long ride to the seaside taking the long road around Milk River, past the mountain, Round Hill and back again.'

'Wow,' he breathed out. 'We'll be going there to climb the mountain. Round Hill as well.'

'Well,' Owen spoke to his friend, 'Josh, if you want to go mountain climbing with them you can just rule me out.'

One of the older guys looked at Owen saying, 'This guy is a chicken.'

Owen Jarvis has always been afraid of heights. In those days it was only the older boys who were allowed to go to the mountain. There were many dangers on the mountain, such as sinkholes. And some of them might be covered by fallen branches and leaves. If anybody should accidentally fall into one of them they might not come out alive. Things were different in those days when Owen was a child. It could be said that those days were the good days in Jamaica, where children's safety was concerned.

CHAPTER 16

CHILDREN OF THE POOR ENVIRONMENT

Despite the children of the village having been born and raised in a poor environment, they were very happy. They had plenty of freedom and lots of places to play. Children in those days were safe to go about on their own. The older boys and girls in the village would have taken care of them even if they weren't family. They would feed them when they were hungry and protect them from falling into trouble. The parents in the village were the same. They would take care of other people's children and treat them just as their own. Owen Jarvis and his brothers and sisters and friends usually played together at his parents' home. The reason for this was that from Owen's home there were clear views of the Caribbean Sea.

CHAPTER 17

A CLEAR VIEW OF THE SEA

At times whenever large ships sailed by, the children seeing them would get excited. They would shout out aloud and wave their hands just for fun because they knew that nobody in the ships would see nor hear them. Young Owen Jarvis and his brothers and sisters used to pretend that they were the musketeers. That meant all for one and one for all. In the village where young Owen Jarvis's parents lived, the older boys would keep an eye on the younger ones. No harm should come to them.

As years wore on, the children grew older. Owen Jarvis was much older now, and he began thinking of his future. His father, Uriah, had passed away at an early age. Since then, the family's future didn't seem so bright, so Owen Jarvis decided to emigrate, and he was now waiting for a date to go to England. One evening before he left Jamaica, he went to pay his Aunt Amanda a visit and say goodbye to her. She said, 'Owen, your Uncle Arran Golding went to England in the early days and we haven't heard from him since then. So when you go to England you should try and find out if he is alive or if he is dead.'

When Owen was on his way home , he came upon some of his friends and they ask him to play a game with them. The game was called "Nearest to Harbour". Cashew nuts were the prize. Then, to Owen's dismay, as soon as it was his turn to play, one of his brothers shouted out, saying, 'Owen, your mum wants you now.'

CHAPTER 18

THE FLIGHT DATE

Owen looked over at his brother in a way that if looks could kill!. Then he said to his friends, 'You continue playing.' He would only be a minute. Then he went off running for home. As soon as he got home, he called, 'Mum, I'm losing all of my cashew nuts and it was my turn to win them back.'

'Well,' she replied, 'if you are losing, now is the right time to stop then you won't lose any more. However,' she said, 'I have good news for you.'

'What good news could that be?' he asked in a sulk.

'Your flight date to England has come through. You will be on a late flight.'

As soon as he heard that, he thought about the time he'd have to leave home for the airport. He'd have to set off very early. The airport in Kingston was several miles away from his home. Owen Jarvis breathed out with a sigh. He didn't want to leave his mother and his brothers and friends. After his father had passed away his mother tried her utmost to keep the family together under the age-old tradition. But without a husband the children's future was looking bleak. After the last World War, the British Government had invited people from West Indian descent to go and live in Britain and work. In those days the war was recently over and the British economy was struggling. Most of the young boys and girls in the village where Jarvis lived were going to England. Some of the girls were going there to study to be nurses. Others were going there to work towards a better way of life.

CHAPTER 19

THE LAST WORLD WAR

Owen Jarvis was 24 years old when he came to live in England. Now that Owen Jarvis had become an adult, the story of his youth days has come to an end.

His granddaughter called out, 'Oh no, Grandad, now that Owen has come back to England a new chapter of his life story has begun.' Now another part of the Owen Jarvis story has begun. The first day he comes to live in Leeds, West Yorkshire!

After the last World War many Jamaican people, both men and women, were prompted by the British government to emigrate to England. There were plenty of jobs for men and women to do. Owen Jarvis was 24 years old when he arrived in Great Britain, having travelled to England on Good Friday.

He had thought that everything would be all right for him in his new country. The very first day he arrived in Leeds, he was ignored by the first person he met. He could feel his heart sink within him. Then, to his dismay, he realised that all those West Indian people who came to Britain in the early days to live and work had suffered a lot of racial abuse. Owen didn't expect that Jamaican people would have been treated with indifference, having been British subjects for many years. It wasn't many days before he found out that black people weren't welcome at certain places in Leeds such as pubs, clubs, some churches and hotels. Despite there being many empty houses and rooms to let, in certain areas there would be a notice on them saying "No blacks, no dogs and no Irish"; they were likening black people to dogs. The Irish were also treated with some kind of racial disdain, but not on the same level as the black people because they were white.

Thanks be to God, as time wore on, Owen Jarvis was able to find out more about the native white people, that some of them were not without humanity and were more accepting to other people's cultures and ways of living. However, as the days wore on, God must have seen how distressed Owen Jarvis was. One night in the late '70s, he went to bed and was woken up again by a long, loud stretch of thunder. Within that stretch of thunder, he heard the voice of the Lord our God. He had spoken though the sounding of the great thunder, saying, 'I am the Lord your God and there is no other God beside me.' That meant that he should stop worrying because God is watching over him.

Next morning, he woke up and got out of bed feeling a great change within himself. He now felt as if he was a new person, different from the night before when he went to bed feeling depressed. All that stress and sorrow had been taken away. Ever since he heard the voice of the Lord God, he had a great urge to go and help those children that he had foreseen making trouble on the street and tell them that they could have a brighter future if they changed their way of life and returned to school and be educated.

After he had accepted Jesus Christ as his Lord and saviour he was baptised in the Apostolic Church of Jesus Christ. And, as the years wore on, he was ordained an Evangelist. Now he felt obligated to do the work that the Lord God wanted him to do. But to do this he would need help. He went and told the vision of God he had to a pastor of the church of Christ Apostolic. He was willing to let him use the church hall, but his church didn't have any hall.

However, on another day he went to see the pastor at the United Reformed Church, which was on Harehills Road, which was not far from where he lived. The pastor's name was Sheila Sandison. She is deceased now, but she was such a friendly, loving pastor. She told him that the only thing she could suggest was that if Owen could take care of the church, he could use the church hall after their service on a Sunday is over. He was so grateful he was lost for words. However, within a few months, some of God's faithful people, a lady of the church known as Mother Williams, a sister in the church known as Sister Banner, and Owen and his wife, Deloris, got together and they were able to buy a second-hand minibus to take the children from home to church and back safely.

Within about six months, Owen Jarvis was able to take up to 70 children from off the street, both white and black children, girls and boys from age five upwards. He was able to use the church hall after school and weekends for the use of the children.

Children don't give collection, so Owen and his wife had a hard time supporting the upkeep of the minibus. In addition to that they had their own children to support, but he knew that God wanted him to do this work. And he believed that He would suffice the needs. God must have wanted him to know that He was well pleased with what they were doing.

To his astonishment, one Saturday night he went to bed and as he went off to sleep, the night seemed to become day. He had now found himself at the church where he was caretaker. While he was there cleaning the church a knock came at the door. He went to answer the door and saw a man standing there. 'Hello, sir, are you Owen Jarvis?'

'Yes,' he replied.

'Well,' he spoke, 'I have a message for you. Tomorrow when you take the children to church do not keep them long because you might have to walk back to your home.'

'Why?' he asked. 'Is something going to happen to the minibus?'

'That's the message I had!' he said and away he went.

CHAPTER 20

GOD LOVES CHILDREN

The next day was Sunday and as usual he took the minibus full of children to church. As soon as they settled down and he was about to pray he heard a voice within me saying, *You were told to take the children home early.*

He acted quickly; he encouraged the children to stand up and prayed for them before leading them back out to the minibus. When they got into the minibus, he prayed again because he thought that they may have an accident. However, by this time he had taken all the children back to their home safely and nothing had happened. 'Thank God,' he breathed out.

Now, while he and his family were on their way back, as soon as they came near Potternewton Park, a gentleman just ran out in front of the minibus and stood in the road saying, 'Stop.'

He had to apply the emergency brake and shouted out loud, saying, 'Man, what are you doing?' he thought that he was trying to kill himself!'

He said, 'Sorry but there's a lady about to give birth on the road.'

'Oh my God,' Jarvis said in astonishment, then he and his wife acted immediately, followed by a passing stranger. They went to help a white lady who was about gave birth on the road. No sooner had they got her into the minibus, she gave birth to a baby boy. Shortly afterwards, the ambulance arrived and took her and her baby to the hospital.

After the ambulance had gone, a man came to Jarvis saying that he was the baby's father. 'Thank you very much,' he said. 'You can leave the minibus with me; I'll tidy it up.' So, Jarvis left the minibus with him, and he and his family walked home.

From that day, Owen Jarvis knew that our Lord God was talking to him. He tried to write his story as a book but, without formal academic education, struggled for many years to become a published author. He heard that some of those young West Indians fellows who came to Britain in the earlier days had to do their national service. Others used to work long hours for very low wages.

Before Owen Jarvis had a family, one evening while he was home alone feeling lonely and depressed, he went out for a stroll along the local park. At this time there weren't many West Indian people living in West Yorkshire, just the one or two. However, while he was strolling along through the park, he came upon another West Indian guy who was much younger than he was. You should have seen the surprise showing on their faces, being so glad to see another West Indian person. They greeted each other and gave their names. Jacob and Owen. Now that they had become friends, they had a long chatter. 'Owen,' Jacob spoke, 'can I ask you a question?'

'Of course,' he said, 'please do, go ahead.'

Jacob said, 'Since you have come to live in Yorkshire, have you got a job yet?'

'Oh, yes,' Owen said. After he had spent a few weeks in the country he got a job with the British Railway engineer. Before Jacob could ask any more questions, he told Jacob that if he was looking for a job, he wouldn't advise him to look at the place where he was working.

'Why not?' Jacob asked.

He replied, saying his first day at work was like spending a first day in hell. As soon as Jacob heard this, he looked up towards the heavens. 'Yes,' Owen said. Had God not give him strength he would have just walk off the job and never returned. Poor Owen Jarvis, he was the only black person among a gang of 11 young white guys who might have never seen a black person face to face before in their life. Some of them were English people and some were Irish. They were ruthless and very rude to Owen.

Jacob heard this, he said that he was not surprised, because he had heard of their bigotry before. Then Jacob began to wonder if all the workplaces would be same. As a matter of fact, they were all taking the piss out of Owen in a jokey kind of a way.

Jacob looked at Owen with sympathy, saying, 'That's a horrible place to work, don't you think so, Owen?'

'Yes,' Owen said, 'that's why I have told you it wasn't the right place for you to seek a job.'

'Owen,' spoke Jacob, 'why don't you tell the foreman what they were saying about you?'

'Sure,' Owen said, 'he was just the same as the others.' After having a long chat with Jacob, it was now time to part company. After Jacob had gone, Owen breathed out, 'Oh my God.' He had forgot to exchange home addresses with Jacob.

CHAPTER 21

HELL'S WORKPLACE

Now to make a bad situation worse, within the passing of a few days, the foreman gave Owen a young Irish guy to be his workmate. Ever since Owen started to work with the guy, he was always trying to measure his strength against Owen Jarvis. They wanted to know how strong the black man is. *Oh my God*, Owen cried within himself, when he found out that he would be working with a very dangerous employee.

One morning at work, Owen and his mate, the Irish guy, went to work with some of the other workers' load, a train trailer with some 60-foot rails. In those days, most of the railway work had to be done by hand, as there wasn't any of the high technology lifting system that they have these days. It took six people using what is known as twiners to lift a 60-foot rail onto the trailer, two people on each. As soon as Owen and his mate has twined up their side of the rail so far off the ground, his mate, the Irish guy, who wanted to know how strong Owen was, suddenly let go of his side of the twiner. Poor Owen Jarvis tried to hold it up but his strength gave way. The twiner spun round quickly and hit Owen Jarvis slightly at the side of his head. He could smell his blood as if his nose was about to bleed. He took a step forward, but he staggered back a little. Ever since he started working with the gang he had taken everything that they had thrown at him but on this day his mate went too far, causing him to become angry with words, almost going into blows.

The other workers cried out, saying, 'Jarvis, are you all right?'

His workmate, the Irish guy, said, 'Owen, I'm sorry it slipped out of my hand.'

If that was the truth or not, after a few weeks had passed, Owen Jarvis' back pain got worse, and he was no longer able to keep that job. After leaving the railway he visited a physician. Within six months he was able to start another job. His new job was a driving job to deliver small articles from one firm to another.

As the years wore on, more black people came to live in West Yorkshire. Owen Jarvis found some more West Indian friends who also loved sports, mostly cricket. But to their resentment, in those days, whenever West Indian international cricketers came to Yorkshire, to Headingley Stadium, he and his friends would stay away because of racial abuse by the English supporters.

CHAPTER 22

A CHANGING COMMUNITY

As years wore on, the future generations of West Indies descent might have brought some diversity into society by having mixed marriages. This is a true saying: there are good and bad in people of every nation. The good news is that Owen Jarvis's children had now become men and women. He and his wife, Deloris, give God thanks. For it is through His mercies that they are alive to see their children grow up and getting married. God be praised. They have now lived to see the best days of their lives.

On the day of their son Isaac's wedding, Owen and Deloris set off to get to the church as early as possible. But they were very frustrated on the way. After all the effort they have made they didn't make it to the church on time. The road was full of traffic and they just couldn't get past.

Unfortunately, when they got to the church, the bride and bridegroom and their guests were already outside in the church garden having their photograph taken. However, they went and greeted their fabulous daughter-in-law.

After having their photograph taken, they all went off to the reception hall. Family and guests had a very wonderful reception party. They could have danced the night away. Jarvis then reminded his wife that their other son would be getting married in three months' time so there was a lot of happy days to come.

CHAPTER 23

MY WINDRUSH FRIENDS

Two weeks later, another of Owen Jarvis's sons got married. He made a promise to himself that at the end of the month he'd go to pay some of his older Windrush Jamaican friends a visit.

After the marriage of his dear beloved son, Calvin, the days wore on quickly. One night, before Owen Jarvis went on his visit, he went to bed hoping he might wake up early in the morning because he didn't like to be late for an appointment. But on this particular morning of his visit, he woke up very late. He sprang up out of bed and looked at the time. 'Oh my God,' he uttered. Then he noticed that his wife, Deloris, was already up and away. She had let him sleep a little longer, seeing as he went to bed late. Jarvis took another look at the clock. He should have been up and away on his visit a long time ago but he had overslept. He immediately got dressed and went downstairs. He went into the kitchen and took a look outside. It looked as if it was going to be a bright sunny day. But he knew that Britain's weather could change in less than no time. He decided to make the best of the morning.

Before he went back up the stairs, he saw one of his sons on his way to the door with his headphones in his hand. 'Dad,' he called, 'I'll catch you later.'

'OK,' his dad said, 'I'll be going out shortly as well, so you try get back before your mother returns.'

'Oh dear,' he uttered sharply, 'Dad, I almost forgot, Mum says that she has taken her keys with her. She will be back soon.' Then he put his earphones over his head and off he went. Owen didn't hesitate; he went out shortly after his son.

From his home in the Yorkshire suburb, it was only a short walk to the first home of his visit. He was going to let the older people know that it would be good for them if they could stay active. Because physical activity can improve health regardless of age, even if it is chronic illness. Because he himself had been suffering from chronic illness which had been helped by activity. He would try his utmost to help others, young or old, so that they might cope with the stress of the days. However, when his visit was over, and he was on his way home, he met his old friend Jacob Roberts. 'Owen Jarvis,' Jacob spoke, 'boy am I glad to see you again!'

'Me too,' Owen Jarvis said. 'Where have you been all these years?'

Jacob said, 'I never thought that I would see you again.' He continued, 'I might be going back to Jamaica soon according to what the government are saying.'

'What are you talking about?' Owen Jarvis asked him, concerned.

Jacob said, 'The government are planning to deport some of us who they call the Windrush Jamaicans.' After saying this he looked at Owen with tears in his eyes and then he walked away sobbing.

CHAPTER 24

THE DISTRESSED MAN

Owen Jarvis found it hard to believe that Jacob has told him the full story. He didn't think for a moment that the government would do such a thing as send those West Indies people who came to Britain in the Windrush days unwillingly back to Jamaica. If Jacob was too young at the time his parents brought him to England, he wouldn't have his own passport. But he had been in the country from a child. Why now? If he should return to Jamaica, to the place of his birth, nobody would remember him. Now Jacob might have wanted to know who he could turn to for help. Owen Jarvis didn't ask him about his parents because it might have added to his sorrow.

CHAPTER 25

A VISITOR ON APRIL FOOLS' DAY

The first day of April is commonly known as April Fools' Day. Owen Jarvis and his wife, Deloris, and their daughter and one of their granddaughters were in the living room that morning tidying up the decorations of Deloris's past birthday. While they were laughing and joking about April Fools' Day, her granddaughter looked through the window, catching sight of a gentleman coming towards the house. 'Granddad,' she called, 'it seems as if one of your Windrush age-group Jamaican friends is coming to the house.' After saying this, she started to laugh. Windrush Jamaican people seemed a funny name to her. Her grandad shared a smile with her. Then he timidly got up from his seat, aided by his walking stick.

He went slowly up to the window and had a look outside. 'Oh my God,' he uttered, surprised. 'That's Jacob.' He paused. He had met Jacob not many days ago and he was very worried about something that he didn't want to talk about. Owen Jarvis had thought that Jacob's problem might have got worse and wanted to talk to someone from his original country. Having all these thoughts, he went off towards the door, walking slowly to meet Jacob.

As soon as he saw Jacob, he noticed that he wasn't walking his usual style of walking. Owen Jarvis saw that Jacob was sad and wanted to make him smile. He stood at the doorway and shouted out to Jacob in his old Jamaican way of talking. 'Boy, why are you looking so sad?' he asked. Jacobs looked at him but didn't even smile. He came to the door and shook hands with Owen. 'What is wrong, Jacob?' asked Owen.

Instead of replying, Jacob went past him with a sad face and went into the living room saying hi to Owen's family and they went into the next room leaving him and Owen to have their chat. Jacob sat for a few minutes looking at Owen then said, 'Owen, do you remember meeting me a few days ago?'

'Yes,' Owen said, 'but you just walked away without telling what was wrong with you.'

He replied saying, 'Don't you know that the government had plotted against those who they call the Windrush Jamaican people?'

Owen looked at him with a smile and said, 'Jacob, what is the plot about?'

He said that the government planned to deport some of those people they called Windrush Jamaican people back to

Jamaica. As soon as Owen heard this, he looked at Jacob again. He had thought that Jacob was trying to catch him out, it being April Fools' Day. He pointed a finger towards the clock and Jacob looked at the time.

'OK,' Jacob said, 'I know that you don't believe me. But my second thought was it might be because of the house shortages. But I heard that there are plenty of empty buildings all over the country that are in need of repair.'

'Yes,' Owen said, 'there are also many homeless people in the country.'

He replied saying that he had always asked himself why the authorities allow the private sector to own them. Now the poorer people had to pay a higher rent which some of them might not be able to pay and might have to sleep out.

As soon as Jacob says this, Owen looked at him again saying, 'Jacob, are you really sure this isn't a joke?'

He replied, saying 'Don't you ever listen to the news?'

Owen said, 'Jacob, the Windrush Jamaica people didn't come to England as immigrants, we came here because we are British subjects.' Then Owen showed him that he had a British passport, saying that it was issued to him by the British Governor Blackburn. Then Owen thought, *What if what Jacob is saying about the plot is true?* It would have brought to light the story of Esther, one of the Bible's characters. Esther's stories, chapter 8–10, tells the story of King Ahasuerus. He didn't know that his prime minister had a secret plot to kill off all the Jews that live in the king's province on the king's birthday. The reality is this, men might have a plot, but God has many of ways to deliver His people.

CHAPTER 26

THE WORRIED MAN

Owen Jarvis came from the West Indies, but he had lived in England for over 50 years. Since then, he hasn't returned to see his parents or his friends. If he were to return there now, he would be penniless. Owen Jarvis didn't want to discourage Jacob but deep in his heart he was sincerely worried as he was also a Jamaican national. Then he thought of the worst day of his life, when his dear mother passed away in Jamaica, and he wasn't able to go and pay her his last respects. Jacob looks at him saying, 'Owen, I am truly sorry to upset you.'

'Oh no, Jacob,' Owen said, 'don't you be sorry.' But in the depth of Owen's soul, he believed that should he ever return to Jamaica, he could picture himself lying on the beach near the Caribbean Sea with a nice cold glass of coconut water beside him, whilst enjoying the clean air coming from the sea.

While he was thinking all these things in his heart, Jacob got up from his seat with a stretch. 'Owen,' he uttered, 'I must be on my way. I'll see you again soon.'

As he was about to go, Owen said, 'Jacob, I almost forgot, my grandchildren have asked me to write a story that is based on Owen Jarvis's boyhood days. And about the place where he was raised up from a child in the West Indies!'

He replied in another way, saying, 'Owen Jarvis, I have noticed that these children born in this country, who the government calls the Windrush generation, are much more radical than we were at their age.'

'Oh, yes,' Owen said, 'that's the truth. They refused to accept people's bigoted remarks against the colour of their skin.'

Before Jacob left he said, 'Owen Jarvis, don't you forget to send me a copy of the book when it is published.'

They had a laugh and he went on his way. After Jacob had gone, Owen said to himself, *the Windrush West Indies children are fully aware that their parents and grandparents were here when the country needed them the most.*

Then Owen's daughter, Leona, said, 'Dad, you can let your friend know that we too have oftentimes been hustled by certain people who had a problem with our colour, so he's not alone. The Windrush people's children know perfectly well that their Windrush parents had done good for the country. Why are they being hustled by the government who should protect them?'

Asked Owen's son, Lee, 'He was allowed to be angry for what has happened to his Dad's friend, Jacob, but he wasn't allowed to let his feelings exasperate others around him.'

They were very angry knowing that their parents had suffered much abuse in those early years when they came to live in West Yorkshire. Now that some people came to their senses they should be ashamed of their past behaviour.

CHAPTER 27

MY COUNTRY BRITAIN

Leona Morton, though, went back to her granddad who had often assured his grandchildren that of all the countries in the world, our country Britain is one of the best to live in. He had also said that not all British people were unsociable to black people, it was just the older one or two. Some of them were very kind, loving, full of humanity and willing to help others whenever they could. She agreed with her granddad because she had lots of friends, many of them white people. She believed that her generation was differently minded from the elders. They see each other as a people and not by the colour of their skin.

CHAPTER 28

THE LADY AND THE SNAKES

One day Leona Morton went to visit her granddad. After she had gone, her granddad, Owen Jarvis, looked at the time. *Well*, he mumbled within himself, *the day has almost been spent.* However, the evening was still bright and sunny so he decided to go for a walk. He now found himself on a high street in the Yorkshire suburb.

He was only a short distance away from his home when he came upon one of the world's most gorgeous young mothers. She was wearing a short summer dress that showed off her beautiful figure. Her long dark hair was blowing in the wind; the most beautiful lady on earth. Her young son was with her; he was just over a year old at the time. As they were going in the same direction, Owen Jarvis walked along with them to a local park. From one word to another Owen Jarvis asked her what her name was. Instead of giving her name she said that she was the daughter of a politician, whom she didn't name.

They went on walking together until they came to a certain place in the park. She chose a spot of grass which was beneath the shadow of a large tree. She took off her coat and hung it onto a lower branch of the tree. Then she sat down with her baby beside her. While she was talking with Owen Jarvis, she didn't notice that her baby wandered away from her. Owen called her, 'Madam, look, your baby has wandered away from you.'

She looked and saw her child a distance away from her. She smiled, and said, 'Jarvis, watch this.' She rested her hand onto her breast and called, 'Baby, it's feeding time.' The baby looked and saw his mother's hand rested on her breast and returned to her in a rush.

Then suddenly the most unexpected happened. The baby bit on his mother's breast and a miracle happened that almost brought tears to Owen's eyes, seeing it happen to such a beautiful young lady and her baby boy. As soon as she child bit the nipple of his mother's breasts, they became heads of snakes and immediately she became a mother cow, and her son became a baby calf. Never in his life had he seen such a dramatic situation. Owen stood at the spot and looked at the cow which not long ago was a beautiful lady. He was dumbfounded. He didn't know what or why this had happened to one of the most beautiful young ladies in the world. She was the daughter of a politician. She had a very handsome-looking child. He could have panicked but he went away with tears in his eyes and sadness in his heart.

CHAPTER 29

THE MYSTERIOUS FLYING LEOPARD

As the days wore on, Owen came upon another mystery that he would never forget. People have oftentimes spoke of the worst days of their lives. You might ask yourself, will such a day ever come in my life? The answer is this: you just cannot tell.

Not many years ago, on the afternoon of a bright summer day, a young man named Dalton Noble found himself camping out with a group of friends at a place they had never gone to before. As the day drew closer towards evening, while others were in the camp doing their thing, Dalton found himself walking alone through dense woodland. As he went on walking suddenly the woodland became very creepy. Things began moving in the undergrowth, which he imagined to be the woodland creatures. Then the trees began shaking heavily when there was no wind blowing. Dalton got scared and began walking timidly, looking back. With every stride he took, his heart beat faster. At length he came upon a large gate which was narrowly open; he squeezed himself through hoping he might come upon someone. Then, to his horror, as soon as he went through, the gate slammed tightly shut behind him. Poor Dalton was scared half to death. He tried to get out again but he couldn't find the way.

While he was walking, looking here and there, he thought of his friends who he had left behind. They might be out looking for him? Poor Dalton Noble wasn't aware that the minute he came through the gate he has been stalked by an angry leopard. Then suddenly he caught sight of the leopard at full speed coming towards him. He took a quick glimpse at the leopard, it was running but its feet weren't touching the ground. 'Oh my God,' he cried, 'I am dead.' He took a quick look around the place but there was no escape. There was a large tree in front of him but he didn't have enough time to climb. The leopard was able to climb as well.

He thought that he might outrun the leopard by running around the tree. But how long could he kept running? He was already breathless. Then, to his relief, a gentleman came and drove the leopard away. Dalton fell to the ground, he was breathless. As soon as he regained his composure, the keeper of hell's gate said to him, 'What are you doing here?' Before he could reply, the keeper said, 'You're lucky to be alive.'

'Yes,' Dalton said, 'thank you very much for rescuing me.'

The gatekeeper said, 'You wouldn't be thankful if you knew what this place is. I'll let you out this time.' Upon saying this he opened the gate and let Dalton out. 'Don't you ever come back here and tell your friends that you have just escaped from hell.'

'Thank you very much, sir,' said Dalton. Now with tears of joy and trembling knees he went off running as fast as he could to get away from that place.

Being excited, he suddenly woke up out of his sleep. Then he realised he was dreaming. He immediately decided to turn his life over to Jesus Christ, since he had escape from hell. Next day, Dalton went to visit his friend to let them know that he was a Christian now and why. On his way, he saw one of his friends talking with a guy called Owen Jarvis. 'Owen, do you ever have something on your mind that will not leave, no matter how hard you try?'

'Oh, yes,' Owen said, 'sometimes it might be a song or it could be many other different things.'

'Of course,' Dalton said, 'I could have written many books from things in my mind.' After he had said this, he and his friend went off saying to Owen Jarvis, 'Catch you later.'

Owen lifted up his hand, saying, 'Goodbye.'

CHAPTER 30

THE SCIENCE PROFESSORS

One evening after school, Leona Morton went to visit her granddad.

After her visit was over and she had gone, her granddad's thoughts went back to the year 1977 when his children were as young as her. One day, his wife, Deloris, took the children to the fair at the park. And while he was on his way to the park, he saw three plant science professors and they foretold him of an Incoming deadly virus.

CHAPTER 31

A TRUE REVELATION

Owen's thoughts went back the 27th of March 1977. He, his wife and family were up and about doing the usual things. At the end of the day and when it was night the family went to bed at their usual time. As the night grew older, the most unexpected thing happened. Owen Jarvis and his wife, Deloris, had a very short rest. As soon as they rested their heads on their pillows and dozed, they woke up again. It was daylight. The morning had grown very quickly. The sun was now blazing through their bedroom window. To them things didn't seem quite right. The night was extra short, and now the day seemed to be likewise.

CHAPTER 32

MYSTERIOUS DAYS

The house in which the family live has four bedrooms upstairs. It was just a few steps away from the road. Owen and his wife Deloris live in the first bedroom. The children were in other rooms. Owen Jarvis was the first to get up out of bed that morning. After getting dressed he went downstairs to the kitchen. He took a look through the kitchen window into the backyard. Nothing had changed. By this time, his wife Deloris had got up out of bed with a stretch and a tired yawn. She went to the bedroom window, looked outside and saw the dazzling light of the sun spread over the multicultural district of Leeds in West Yorkshire. Her eyes lit up seeing it was going to be a beautiful sunny day in Britain where the weather has always been draggy.

She went quickly to the children's room. She knocked on the door. 'Wakey, wakey, children, are you waken?' she asked. But she had no reply. The children heard their mother calling but they didn't want to get out of bed so they pretended to be asleep. But she was quite aware of the children's tricks. She uttered the magic words, 'I'll be going to the park today. I heard that the fairground is open.'

No sooner had she mentioned going to the fair the children sprang up out of bed. 'I am going with you,' said one.

'Me too,' said the other.

'OK,' she said, 'as soon as we've had our breakfast we'll be on our way.'

After breakfast Deloris went back up the stairs. While she was on her way, a knock came to the front door. 'Children,' she called, 'will one of you answer to the door?'

'OK, Mum,' replied her son, Darren. He didn't hesitate; he went to the door and saw a young lady named Meg standing there. 'Mum,' he calls, 'your friend Meg is here for you.'

Deloris hung her head over the banister. 'Hi, Meg,' she said, 'you're just in time, I was just about taking the children to the park!'

'That's great,' Meg said. 'Can I come along with you?'

'Of course, dear,' Deloris said. 'We would be delighted. Won't we?' she asked the children. But instead of replying they looked at her with a giggle. 'Children,' Deloris spoke, 'let us go and say goodbye to your father.'

Their father, Owen, was at this time in the dining room. The children went and gave him a hug and his wife gave him a kiss saying, 'My friend Meg and I are taking the children to the park, we'll try not to be late back.'

'OK,' he replied.

She kissed him saying, 'See you later.' Then they went off through the front door and away. Owen was now home alone.

The day had grown much older and it seemed to be that his wife and Meg and the children had been gone for many hours.

The children were having great fun at the fair. Owen Jarvis was at home thinking, had his wife gone to the inner-city shopping area to catch a bus to the park? He was very worried about his family at the park. Every minute he would take a look at his wristwatch and have a peep through the window. The inner-city parade wasn't far from his home; it was just at the top of the street. At certain times of the day it would get very crowded. There were two large supermarkets, one on either side of the road with a layout similar to a junction that is controlled by traffic lights, so that pedestrians were able to cross safely from one supermarket to the other. The area has been lately modernised. The main road that led towards the national park also passed by the inner city. The old landmarks, such as the old cinema, were still there. On the opposite side of the road was an old public house. People used to go there and have their lunch and sit outside in summer months. There was a bank and a post office, and on the upper side of the road was a church a distance away. There were also many local businesses in and around the area.

Owen's thoughts now went back to his wife and children, that they might be on their way now walking from the park. The day had grown much older. It had been many hours since Deloris and Meg and the children had gone to the fair. Owen was worried because there wasn't an occasion in which his wife kept the children so long at the park. He looked at his watch again. 'Oh, boy,' he mumbled to himself. He was now tired of waiting so he decided to go to the park and see what was keeping them.

CHAPTER 33

THE SPARE LAND

No sooner had he walked to the end of the avenue in which he lived, when he saw three well-dressed white males standing looking at a section of spare land, which was on the other side of the lane. His immediate though was that they were surveying a new development site. There was a shortage of houses in the area. However, while Owen was passing by, one of the gentlemen shouted, 'Hello.' He took a look around but there wasn't anybody else there.

By this time, one of the gentlemen came to him saying, 'Mister, do you know who this piece of spare land belongs to?'

Before Owen answered he thought about it for a moment then he said that he wasn't too sure, but it might belong to the church over there. He pointed. While he was talking to the first gentleman, two of his colleagues came and said hi to him. The oldest of the three men probably was in his 60s. He was about six feet tall, slimly built, dark hair and clean-shaven. The other two men were much younger than he was. The older of the three men gave his name as Professor Clinton White. He was the head professor of plant science at a private university in the city which wasn't far away. Professor Clinton White said that he and his two colleagues were looking for an extremely rare plant and it was very important that they find it quickly or else many people were going to die of an incoming virus. They were also looking for extra volunteers help them find the plant quickly.

As soon as Owen heard that they were looking for volunteers, he looked at the time. He told the professors that it was getting late. He was on his way to meet his wife and children. So he promised the professors that if they were still there when they returned they could tell him what the search was all about. The professors agreed and he went off, taking vigorous strides until he came to another road at the bottom of the lane. Surprise, surprise, he looked a distance ahead and caught sight of a young lady who looked like his wife coming towards him. *Wait a minute*, he uttered within himself. If she was his wife where were the children and her friend. Meg?

He went on walking until they got much closer. 'Deloris,' he called out, 'where are the children and your friend, Meg?' She waved her hand as if to say wait until she got closer then she'd tell him. He was very annoyed not seeing the children with her, but he didn't shout at her in the street. He stood still and waited until she caught up to him.

'Well,' she spoke, 'I met your cousin, Janet, at the park, she asked if she could take the children home with her for an hour or so. She said that she will bring them back before night. And my friend Meg didn't stay long at the park, she went home early.' Owen thought that she shouldn't have left the children behind. It was a ridiculous idea. She got angry with him saying, 'Listen to me, Owen Jarvis, don't you put the blame on me. It was your Janet who took the children. I can't see anything wrong with that.'

They came into the lane where the professors were searching for the uncommon plants. 'Professors,' Owen calls, 'we are back now, you can finish telling us what you were saying to me before.' The professor came and shook hands with Deloris and introduced his two colleagues. They said hi to her.

'Well,' the professor said, 'we were telling your husband about an incoming virus that carries a very deadly strain of which there is no immediate antidote. Unless we find a plant known as the uncommon plant to make up a multipurpose antidote quickly, many people are going to die.'

'May the Lord help us,' cries Deloris, frightened.

CHAPTER 34

THE UNCOMMON PLANT

Deloris turned towards her husband saying, 'Owen, are you willing to go and help the professors search for the plant tomorrow?'

'Sure,' he said, 'I'd be honoured.'

Now while Owen and Deloris were on their way home, he looked sharply at her, saying, 'Deloris, how can the professors make up a multipurpose antidote when he doesn't know what kind of a strain the virus might bring forth?'

She replied, 'That's why he's making it a multipurpose antidote.' Then she took hold of his hand and said, 'Darling, I'm happy that you've agreed to be a volunteer.'

He said, 'It's because it is for a good cause.

CHAPTER 35

HE HASN'T A CLUE

Despite Owen Jarvis having agreed to be a volunteer helper, in his heart he hadn't got a clue as to what the uncommon plants might look like.

Next morning, bright and early, Owen Jarvis found himself at the professors' private university in the city. There were many other volunteer workers waiting for the professor who had not arrived yet. They didn't have to wait long. The professor came riding on a bike. He was in a rush to get to the lab; unfortunately, all of his experimental results had gone to complete shambles. And he was absolutely furious with himself. Now he was in greater urgency to find the uncommon plant. He called the students to attention. It was time for him to explain what this extraordinary, uncommon plant looked like. He told the students that he had seen the plants only once and that was when he was a boy. Now he was over 60 years old.

'Will such a plant still exist?' one student asked.

While the student was waiting for an answer, the professor swivelled his chair around to face them. Instead of replying to the student's question, he asks them to pack their belongings. He would be taking them to the library. They were going to research the older books. One of them might tell them more about the unknown plants.

The students immediately took up their belongings and off they went with the professors to the library, which was on the university premises but a distance away from where they were. Once they arrived at the library the professor would tell the students which books to search to find the plant. If they found the correct book it would have details of the plants they were looking for. It might even have a picture of it, he thought.

By this time the day has grown much older. They had searched for many hours through hundreds of books. Officially the class should have been over but the students decided to work overtime knowing that it was a life-or-death situation. At length the professor came upon an ancient, years-old diary. It was hidden in a corner on the shelf. He brushed it against his trousers. Then began to flick the pages over one by one. The diary was very old, and the pages were thin and very fragile. The students stood excitedly, holding their breath, looking at him. Suddenly they saw a big smile appear on the professor's face. And they all cried out joyfully, saying, 'Yes! The professor has found it.' He flicked the page and saw a brilliant photograph of the uncommon plant. It was among some of the other weird plants on the same page! The professor showed the students the plant, saying, 'This is what you'll be going to look for in the morning.' He then told the students that the plant had a nickname: the American grass pad plant.

CHAPTER 36

THE FARMERS

Now that they had found a picture of the plants, it was time for them to go and search for it. Next day, bright and early, Professor Clinton send out two groups of students to two different places to search for the plant. The students were told that if they didn't find the plant quickly, many people were going to die of the incoming virus. The first group of students that he selected was Ricky and Willy Houston. The second group was Geoffrey Watson, Owen Jarvis and Jennifer Winter, who was one of the professor's granddaughters. They went off, following the professor's directions.

At length they came upon a farm, which was on the outskirts of the city. The students got there just in time as the farmer and her two sons were just about to leave. She was very excited to see the students because students didn't often come to her field! 'Well, well,' she said, 'what has brought you lot here?'

Ricky was the spokesperson. He gave his name then he gave the others' names. He told the farmer that they were looking for a very strange, uncommon plant. And its nickname, American grass pad plants. As soon as Ricky mentioned the American grass pad plant, the lady farmer looks at them and had a laugh. She had never heard of such a plant before. However, she took the students to her farmhouse and showed them a sample of all different kinds of seeds that she had in store, saying they were the only seeds that she had.

As soon as she said this, one of her sons called out, saying, 'Mummy, my brother and I might have seen the plant that the students are looking for!' They didn't wait for an answer; as soon as he spoke, he and his brother ran off at full speed through fields of corn. About ten minutes later they return with two bundles of plants and gave them to the students, saying, 'You can take these to the professors.'

The students took the two bundles of plants from the boy and thought of the photograph that the professors had previously shown them. It wasn't similar. But they decided to take them to the university to be examined by the professors.

CHAPTER 37

THE WORM BREEDING PLANTS

When the students arrived at the university, Professor Clinton White was in the lecture room. They went to the door, knocked and called, 'Professor.' As soon as the professor heard his name, he came out of the lecture room as quick as a flash.

'Have you found the plant?' he asks excitedly. Ricky handed him the two bundles of plants that had been fetched from the farm. The professor took them. After taking a close look at them, he said, 'These aren't the right plants.' He told the students to follow him to the laboratory to take a closer look at them. After he had examined the plants, he said, 'Students, you have fetched me what known as the worm breeding plant. Would you like me to prove it to you?'

They answered, 'Yes, Professor.'

He untied a bundle of the plants and gave each student a branch. One brave student spoke up and said, 'Professor, what shall we do with the plants?'

'Just keep hold of them until I return,' he replied. He told the students that they should hold the plants, he would be back in five minutes' time.

Then, to the students' horror, as soon as the professor had gone, the plants suddenly decayed in their hands. Then thousands of baby worms began to breed from the decayed plants. Never before had they seen anything grow as fast as those worms. Then they became very vicious, nipping at everything in the way while crawling up the walls and running about on desks and falling to the floor. In less than no time there were thousands of angry worms in the lab. The students soon got scared and started to run out of the university, brushing and stamping. Some cried out loud saying, 'There're worms on our clothes.'

At this point the other groups of students returned, seeing students running outside of the university. The professor's granddaughter who was with the students who had just returned was wondering what was going on, until she heard one student shouting out saying the worms were out of control. At this time the professor was in the building trying his utmost to calm down the students, but he couldn't. The professor's granddaughter outside was concerned for the safety of her granddad, she was trying to go back into the building, but some passing stranger held her back and called for the emergency services.

Within five minutes the fire brigade and the police arrived together. The students were lucky that they were not bitten by the worms. But they were afraid that the professor might be trapped inside and might not come out alive. Within the space of ten minutes, they saw the fire brigade people come out with the professor and his two colleagues and they clapped their hands that they had come out safely. Now that they could see that the professors were all alright, all the students were allowed to go home. But some of the officers remained at the university to investigate the cause of the explosion that followed. The plant science professors and the students didn't find the uncommon plants that day, so they weren't able to make the antidote. But there would be many more incoming viruses, so the search continued for the plants. On July 27th, 1977, Owen Jarvis was one of the students working with the professors who were trying to find a cure for the incoming virus.

CHAPTER 38

COVID-19

The 27th July 1977 might seems many years ago but that was the date Owen Jarvis came upon the three plant science professors. Clinton White was the head professor that predicted the incoming virus for which there isn't any immediate antidote. He said that the virus would cause many deaths before a cure was found.

Now, after all those years, came the deadly Covid-19. It had caught the whole world off-guard. Could Covid-19 be that virus Professor Clinton White had foretold? He had foretold that the virus will take many people's lives before a cure is found and so it had. People of this generation had not experienced a virus like Covid-19 that had taken so many people's lives. People have oftentimes spoken of governments, those of rich countries – they have many great scientists and men of high technology who are able to make rockets and send them to the moon and back again. People in poorer countries cannot believe that the rich had allowed the Covid-19 virus to get out of control before they found a cure. Covid-19 first appeared in China on 3rd December 2019, so it was told. Many people might have asked themselves, why did China keep it quiet for so long before letting other countries know of it, until it got out of control? Then it was made known. Many governments ignored their scientists' reports, saying that it is just a common flu.

It wasn't until February 2020 that some governments started to find a cure for Covid-19. That had given the virus time to spread worldwide. There were many worried people abroad wanting to return to their country with only a short time to catch their flight. Covid-19 was about to cause flights to shut down. Travelling from country to country was coming to an end. Many passengers would be left stranded in another country and separated from their family. Especially those who had parents with poor health. Christmas 2020 was not far away. Some people with poor health were already suffering from being home alone. Now Covid-19 was about to add more to their distress. British people are people of humanity and so they would try their best to help each other the best they could but could only do so much. Some people were already suffering loneliness for many years and might not be able to cope being home alone. Some might not be able to be home alone even for a day before they got stressed. This was not an experience to be disregarded.

Owen Jarvis was at home in bed one night when he heard an old lady in distress crying out loud in a frightened voice saying, 'I am lonely.' After he had heard the cry of the lonely person he got up and sat on his bed for a few minutes, but he didn't hear her crying voice again. He might have heard it on the radio. He had often left the radio on and went off to sleep.

Then on the 12th of February, while he and his family were at home under Covid-19 lockdown, a letter came through the door. It was from the hospital saying that his appointment has been cancelled. 'Oh my God,' he said, 'the virus must be getting worse.' At this point nobody had thought that Covid-19 would have spread so quickly. It had now become a pandemic. The question was this: had Covid-19 come to cleanse the world of having too many human beings? The winter months of December 2020 were to come. Soon it would be Christmas. Would the country remain under lockdown until then? Family might not be able to visit their loved ones. Children might be not able to visit their grandparents at Christmas. Some of the older parents knew perfectly well that their sons and daughters that lived abroad would not be able to visit them because of their poor health. There would be many heartbroken people, despite advanced technology that enables communication over long distances, such as video calls, the physical absence of their children would still cause emotional pain for these parents. One stranger commented saying, 'Why is such a rich country taking so long to find a cure for Covid-19 virus?'

CHAPTER 39

THE UNSEEN KILLER

On the 15th of January 2020, it was told that the Covid-19 virus had killed over two million people and counting. Yet the authorities still hadn't found a cure for the deadly virus. Why is it that they had taken so long? There are many rich and powerful countries that could have spent millions competing against each other to be the greatest. While humanity's health is ignored? You may ask yourself why thousands of people had to die before a cure was found to stop the deadly virus Covid-19? To all those who put their hope in the Lord Jesus, the 25th of December is to remind everybody of God's son Jesus Christ's birthday. His presence will give light through the dark hours of all those who believe in Him. God can give His people comfort in many different ways.

One day while Owen Jarvis and his family were at home under lockdown from Covid-19, Owen Jarvis had a phone call from his sister, Susan, who he named "lady of the west". She has always given her brother and his family good encouragement throughout the Covid lockdown so they wouldn't feel alone. She has always been a kind, loving, courageous person to the family. She told her brother that it was better to stay indoors and keep alive than to go out and catch the virus and die.

CHAPTER 40

FAMILY GETTING TOGETHER

Owen Jarvis's thoughts went back to the day his daughter finished her university course. The family got together to celebrate. Afterwards they had their photograph taken at the table. Owen Jarvis didn't know how this really happened but later that evening, after his visiting family had gone, a mystery happened.

CHAPTER 41

A WINTER HOLIDAY

Owen Jarvis and his wife and three of their grandchildren were getting ready to go on a winter holiday. Then, to their surprise, just as they were about to leave home, one of the children shouted out, 'Granddad, it has started to snow!' And so it started slowly, and then it came down in much larger flakes. In less than no time, the ground was thickly covered. Owen and his family now found themselves at their cousin Jessica's home in Manchester. They were waiting there until the snow stopped falling and they could be on their way.

By this time, most of the country was thickly covered with snow. Manchester was by far the worst. However, while they were there waiting, Deloris looked sharply at him saying, 'Owen Jarvis, do you think it's a good idea going on holiday at the seaside in this weather?'

'Well, my dear,' he said, 'it might be an experience for us and our children but if you are worried about leaving home why not ask your friend, Miss Johnson, to keep an eye on our place until we return?'

Now Owen Jarvis is a person who has the unusual gift of prophecy. He had been led by the spirit of his vision to go to the seaside. There was something there to be revealed to him. Furthermore, by going there his family would be having a new experience. His wife thought of the situation and became sulky. She got up from her seat in a sulk and went to the door, and saw the children playing in the

snow. She said, 'If the children can be playing outside in the snow, we might as well be on our way. Children, come and say goodbye to your cousin Jessica, we're ready to go.'

As soon as the children heard this, one of them shouted out, 'Yippee!'

The other cried out, 'Yes!'

Jessica looks at Deloris, seeing she was somewhat annoyed with her husband. 'Deloris,' Jessica said, 'can I ask you a question?'

'Of course,' she said.

'Why do you wait until the winter months to go on your holiday?' Instead of replying, Deloris gave her husband the usual look. Jessica knew straight away that it wasn't Deloris's idea. Then Jessica looks at Deloris, saying, 'When you go to the seaside whereabouts will you be staying?'

'Well,' spoke Deloris, 'we'll be going to the north coast. We hope that we might find a private accommodation there.'

Now, seeing as the children were already outside playing in the snow, it was time for them to be on their way. It might be very cold on the beach but the children would have a holiday they would never forget.

CHAPTER 42

THE COLD, SNOWY BEACH

As the days passed on, Owen Jarvis noticed that Deloris was very happy seeing her grandchildren playing on the cold winter beach. She should keep her eyes on them while they played; deep down in Owen's heart he knew perfectly well that this world wasn't a very safe place.

However, after the passing of a few weeks, the snow had melted away but it was still very cold. Within a few days, Deloris has found a new friend by the name of Emily Scot. She and her friend could chat while keeping an eye on the children having fun playing on the cold beach. So far, so good; the family were happy. Owen was very glad.

Next day, bright and early, Deloris and her friend, Emily Scot, went for a walk to the beach taking the children with them. Now that Owen was home alone, and it was still early in the morning, he went back to bed for a longer rest. Owen was a person who had the unusual gift of precognition; he was able to visually detect some unusual disease that kills elephants in a hayfield. While he was in bed, he heard an elephant yell out in a way that suggested it was in great pain. After he had heard the elephant's cries, he got up and sat at the side of his bed to listen. Within the space of three minutes the elephants yelled out again and continued to yell every three minutes. The neighbour's dogs started barking. Owen looked and saw some residents looking in the direction where the sound was coming from. It was coming from a hayfield that wasn't far from the resort area.

He decided to go to the field and see why the elephants were yelling out in such a way. As soon as he got to the hayfield, he reminded himself that he had left the door of his residence open. *It's OK*, he said to himself. His wife might return before him. He looked around the hayfield. 'Oh my God,' he breathed out in astonishment. Some of the elephants were very sick on their feet and trembling. But not for long; they all went silent. Then they all fell to the ground and died. This was a very scary situation; why had the elephants all died so quickly? Owen took a look around the area but there wasn't anybody else to be seen. So he went and took a timid look at one of the dead elephants. There wasn't any blood or bruise or mark on it that he could say could be the cause their death. This was quite a puzzling situation. Then while he was standing there afraid, he heard footsteps. Somebody else was approaching the hayfield. He wasn't sure who it was. Afraid for his safety he went and hid himself among some tall grass in the field. Then he saw a vet coming to help the elephants. He came out of hiding. 'Doctor,' he called to the lady, saying, 'it seems that you've come too late. The elephants have all died now.'

'I'm sorry,' she said, 'I came as quickly as I could when I heard that the elephants were sick.'

Then she went to examine the dead elephants. When she returned, she said that elephants had died of a very unusual disease, which they had caught between the feet.

Owen said, 'I'm very sorry that the elephants have died in such a short space of time.'

After the vet had diagnosed the cause of the elephants' death, she left the hayfield. Owen Jarvis also went off walking slowly. As soon as he went a short distance away from the hayfield he looked ahead and saw his wife running towards him with her eyes full of tears. His heart sank, his immediate thought was that something had happened to the children. He waved his hands and his wife acknowledged him but still came running towards him. He likewise quickened his stride and his wife came running into his arms. 'My darling,' he spoke, frightened.

'What is wrong? Has something happened to the children?'

'Oh no,' she said, 'the children are OK.' She had left them with her friend, Emily. She then rested her head on Owen's shoulder. He dried the tears from her eyes.

CHAPTER 43

A PUDDLE IN THE STREET

She spoke softly through her tears saying, 'One of my friends has told me that while we have been away someone has broken into our house and left it in a terrible state.'

'Take it easy, dear,' said Jarvis. He knew perfectly well that there wasn't much of value left in the house.

Shortly after they had received the message, they found themselves at home again. When Deloris looked and saw the damage that the thieves had left behind, she was dumbfounded. 'Honestly!' she spoke. 'Enough is enough.'

Owen said, 'Let us call the police.'

As soon as he said this, their friend, Miss Johnson, said that she had already called for the police. Within five minutes the police arrived along with the fire brigade. They too were astonished to see what the thieves had done. They had meddled with the gas meter and left the premises to fill with gas. They had also deliberately damaged the water pipes leaving water running through the house making a puddle in the street. The electric meter, which they had tampered with, was sparking. The fire brigade acted quickly, making the premises safe, and left the police to investigate the crime. One officer asked Owen and his wife to make a statement and if they knew of anyone who would be the most likely to do these things to them. But they couldn't think of anyone, so the police investigation continued.

CHAPTER 44

MADELYN DORSEY

Six months later, Leona, one of Owen Jarvis's granddaughters, went to visit him. Returning, she began thinking that she should have stayed little longer to hear her granddad read the first chapter of his mysterious story. She had thought that her granddad had had a long tiresome day and at end of the day she didn't want to spoil his rest. She didn't know this but as soon as she had gone, her granddad started to read the story to himself.

So, the story begins: Once upon a time, not long ago, a young man named Owen Jarvis returned from work at the end of the day and when it was night, he and his wife and young members of the family went off to bed. Then, to their bewilderment, as soon as Owen rested his head onto his pillows it seems that the night became day. Owen now found himself walking a high street not far from home.

He came upon a young, depressed mother by the name of Madelyn Dorsey, a very beautiful young mother. Her son, William, was with her. He was about 12 years old at the time. Before Madelyn became a depressed person, she and her family used to live a happy and exciting life. Then as time wore on, to her shock, one night she and her boyfriend had a break-up. Madelyn had oftentimes asked herself where she went wrong that caused her love life to end up in this way? Now her boyfriend had left her and her son without a home and not a penny in the bank. Madelyn didn't have a job at the time and her income was very low. Poor Madelyn.

One day her landlord gave her notice to quit her tenancy because she couldn't afford to pay her rent. Now she didn't have a place to live. She took her son with her to the local park. Her son went off to play and she sat on the park bench with her head hanging and eyes filled with tears. She was depressed not knowing where she and her son will find a place to sleep that night. The day grew older and older. She now began thinking that she must find somewhere for her son to sleep even for the night. She tried her utmost but seeing as she didn't find a place, she decided to leave her son with a woman she knew not much about. She loved her son very much and hated to leave him with the stranger but she was desperate. She was going to find new accommodation but she couldn't take William with her at the time because she couldn't be sure where she would be sleeping that night. However, before she went, she made a promise with her babysitter, Mrs Carr, that as soon as she found a place for her and William to stay, she would come back for him. She gave Mrs Carr some money to care for William until her return.

William was very unhappy to hear this because he had never been fostered out before. Mrs Carr didn't have any children of her own so William was very uncomfortable staying with her. She showed William a horse saying, 'William, if you promise to behave yourself, I'll give you this horse to keep.'

He loved the horse and called it Purdy, oftentimes he would sit on the grass field talking with the horse as if it was a person. Then unfortunately many weeks had passed, and William's mother, Madelyn, hadn't returned to collect him. The money that she gave Mrs Carr for William's upkeep has been spent. Mrs Carr now became aggressive to William.

Owen's granddaughter said that she could just imagine what young William was going through being left with Mrs Carr, as she went out leaving him alone to sleep in her barn with her animals. That night, William cried and called for his mum until he fell asleep.

CHAPTER 45

THE CRUEL BABYSITTER

Next day early in the morning, Mrs Carr went to the barn to see if William was still there. She didn't send William to school, neither did she allow him to play with other children in the neighbourhood.

Then, on another night, she and her friends went out again, leaving William to sleep in the barn. During the night William timidly opened the barn door and trotted off carrying nothing with him just the horse that Miss Carr gave him. Nobody knew exactly how this really happened but William left Gwent sometime during the night on his own and found himself in a West Yorkshire district, which was about 300 miles away from Gwent.

Owen Jarvis, being a light sleeper, woke up in the early morning by the sound of the animal feet going through the street. He got up out of bed quickly and went to the window. He pulled back the long curtains and had a look outside. He caught sight of a young boy of about 12 years old pulling a horse on a lead made of string. 'Deloris,' he called to his wife, 'please come and take a look at this.'

She hastily got out of bed and went to the window, seeing the young boy leading a horse going through the street. 'Oh my God,' she spoke, 'where could he be going at this time in the morning?' Jarvis looked at the clock it was past four o'clock in the morning. He said he might be running away from home. 'Let us call the police,' said Deloris.

'Not yet,' he said. 'Let us engage him first. You go downstairs and talk with him and then we can call the police.' By doing so they would know that the boy would be safe with them. Thinking of the time in which we live, children aren't safe walking alone at that time of the morning. They just couldn't leave the boy alone in the street.

Deloris got dressed quickly and went downstairs to the door. 'Hello, young man,' she called, and so that the boy might not be afraid, she didn't attempt to go towards him. She stood still at the door. She noticed that he was a very scared child, so she waited to see if he would come to her willingly.

The boy delayed for a while and then he began walking slowly toward her, pulling his horse behind him. As soon as the boy walking towards her she went to meet him. She gave him a motherly hug and took him inside the house. He was hungry and very cold. She left the boy inside the house and took his horse to the back yard and tied it up to a pole then went back into the house. She told the boy her name was Deloris Jarvis. Then she asked him if he had a name.

'Yes,' he replied, 'my name is William Beret.' This he said through his tears and with quivering lips.

Deloris comforted him again, saying, 'William, please do not cry, you can tell me what is wrong and where are you coming from and where were you going to.' He didn't reply, so Deloris went to the kitchen and made William something to eat and drink and gave his horse some of her children's cornflakes with milk.

CHAPTER 46

THE BOY FROM GWENT

 The day has grown much older now. Deloris's son, who was a little older than William, came to talk with him. A few minutes later, Deloris's young daughter, who was about the same age as William, also came and sat with him on the settee. Deloris told her daughter that William had a horse outside in the back yard. 'Wow,' she gasped, excited, 'can we go and have a look at it?'

'Yes,' William said, 'I'll come along with you.' He got up and went with her. She let the horse have a walk round the yard.

When the fussing was over, they went back inside. William was much happier now, seeing other children of his own age group. As soon as they came in and sat down Owen said, 'William, can I ask you a question?'

'Yes,' he replied.

'Can you tell us whereabouts you came from and where you were going?'

William looked at him and, then he looked at his wife with sadness in his eyes as if was about to cry. Then he said, 'I came from Gwent, my mum had left me with a woman named Mrs Carr. My mum promised her that she would come back for me as soon as she found a place for us to stay.

But many weeks passed, and she didn't return. So I'm looking for my mum.'

As soon as he said this, Deloris turned her frightened eyes and looked at her husband, saying, 'Owen, whereabouts in the world is Gwent?'

He answered Deloris, saying, 'Are you asking me whereabouts is Gwent?'

'Yes,' she replied. He says that he isn't too sure, but he thinks Gwent might be somewhere in Wales.

As soon as he said this, his wife went speechless. She couldn't have thought that William could have walked all the way from Gwent to Leeds in West Yorkshire in such a length of time. Now that they had listened to what William said about his mother, they decided that they should give William over to the police and let them take him back to Mrs Carr's home in Gwent. And then they could find out where William's mother has gone to. Deloris was a lady of sympathy, she thought that by this time Mrs Carr might be very worried about where William has gone to. She might have already reported him missing to the police.

As soon as she picked up the telephone and was about to dial 999, William cried out pleading, 'Please, Mrs Jarvis, do not give me over to the police. I want to stay here with you! Please!'. She put down the telephone and asked William why he wanted to stay with her. He replied, 'The police will take me back to Mrs Carr's home.' He didn't want to go back there.

CHAPTER 47

THEY CALL FOR THE POLICE

As the morning grew, one of Deloris's granddaughters came to visit her and saw William crying. 'What is wrong with him?' she asked.

Deloris said, 'He has run away from his carers and doesn't want to go back. Neither does he want us to give him to the police.'

'Please, Grandma,' she pleaded, 'do not give him over to the police yet.'

Deloris in sympathy changed her mind. Then she made a promise to William that if he stopped crying, she would take him back to Gwent herself and make sure that he was safe.

As soon as her husband heard her say this he turned and sharply looked at her saying, 'Did you just say that you'll take William back to Gwent?'

'Yes,' she replies, 'I'll take him and two of the children with us.' By taking her children with her, William might feel more comfortable, having children of his age group travelling with him.

'Are you sure about this?' Owen asked.

'Yes,' Deloris said, 'I'm very sure.'

Deloris decided that when she got to Gwent she would go and see Mrs Carr herself and have a chat with her. If she didn't want to keep William, then she would give him over to the police. When William heard that he would be going back to Gwent he covered up his face and started to cry.

'My poor dear,' Deloris said, 'William, please don't cry. You'll be all right, trust me.' Then she thought that Mrs Carr might be a person who isn't fond of children and might be glad that William had run away. She asked William if his mother told him whereabouts she was going to find a place for them to live.

'No,' William said, but one night while his dad, Michael, and his mother were having a quarrel, he heard his mother packing her things as if she was going to leave.

Then his father said to her 'What about William?' As if he was something borrowed and ready to be handed back.

This he spoke with quivering lips and a trickle of tears fell from his eyes. As soon as he said this, Deloris took hold of his hand, hushing him to stop him crying. She now realised that it was after William's dad had gone that his mum had left him with Mrs Carr and went to find a new place for them to live. But why had his mother not returned? She told William not to worry as she would make sure that the police would find his parents for him.

Now, while they were on their way to Gwent, the day had grown much older. Deloris had been driving on the motorway for many hours. She found a safe place and stopped to read her map because she had never gone to Gwent before. Then she found out that she was almost there and set off driving again. At length they came into Gwent. 'William,' Deloris called, 'do you think you'll able to find Mrs Carr's farmhouse as we drive around, or direct me to the place where your parents used to live before?' To her horror William could remember neither the road on which Mrs Carr lived, nor the place where his parents used to live before. However, Deloris decides to drive around and ask directions.

Now by following a direction given to her by a stranger she came to the last bus stop before the bridge. After crossing over the bridge, the road went on to the countryside. Mrs Carr's farmhouse was the last house on the right-hand side of the road before heading in the countryside. There was a local shop on the opposite side of Mrs Carr's home. It was set aside a T-junction in which one of the roads led beneath the bridge.

CHAPTER 48

THE GWENT DISTRICT

William now recognised the place and pointed the Carr's farmhouse out to Deloris. 'Are you sure that is her?' Deloris asked William.

He said, 'I am quite sure!'

'OK,' Deloris said, 'I'll drive to that side of the road beside Mrs Carr's house.'

'Mum,' uttered her son, Isaac, 'can I go with William to Mrs Carr's home?'

'Oh no,' she said, 'but you can follow him to the gate and wait for him there.'

William took the pony with him, followed by Isaac. As they got to the gate. William looked and saw Mrs Carr stood at her window looking out. William tried to pull the horse in to her gate but it sat down on the road and braced itself against William. Deloris's daughter, Naomi, saw how stubborn the horse was and she went and gave it a stroke as if she was stroking a dog until at length it got up and followed William. Isaac and Naomi followed William and waited at the gate.

As soon as William went inside, Naomi went across the road to the local grocer shop and her brother went back to his mum in the jeep. Isaac looked through the window of the jeep, catching sight of William in Mrs Carr's house standing at the window with a towel in his hand. She had written the time on the towel that Mrs Carr would see Deloris. Then Deloris and her children sat waiting for the time.

She heard some people getting excited on the road beneath the bridge. Then suddenly they saw a police officer giving someone chase. The person he was chasing ran beneath the bridge. As soon as the officer went beneath the bridge, a group of angry young men passing Mrs Carr's place threw something dangerous at the Carr farmhouse, but it missed and rolled on beneath the bridge. The officer didn't know this, but the bridge was about to be blown up. Deloris got out of the jeep quickly. 'Officer,' she called, 'come from under the bridge.' But sadly, the officer wasn't able to get out in time. Suddenly the bridge went up with a bang. November the 17th 2007 had ended in terror for the young police officer who had died.

Jarvis suddenly woke up out of his dream with a fright. It wasn't until he heard his wife and children talking downstairs that he breathed out, saying, 'Thank you, my God, for you have made all these things to be a Revelation.' Then Jarvis thought of the many children all over the world that had been abused by those who should be taking care of them, it was as if he could have heard abused children crying out for help. After a few weeks had passed, Jarvis's thoughts went back to the explosion that he had heard at Governments House in October 1985.

CHAPTER 49

THE EXPLOSION

One morning in October 1985, Owen Jarvis and his family found themselves sat in their living room looking after the children while they watched their favourite programme on the television. Then suddenly a news flash came on. There was an explosion at Governments House this morning. 'Oh my God,' Owen breathed out, frightened. Then they showed the scene of the explosion on the TV. There were ambulances, fire brigade and police officers and other people working at the scene freeing those people trapped in the rubble. The buildings were in complete wreckage. As soon as Owen regained his composure, he jotted down the date of the explosion which was on 10th October 1985.

CHAPTER 50

A VISIT TO THE WEST

The person who was reading the news said that many heads of state from other countries were sending their sympathy to the governments of the country in which the explosion happened. The next day, one of Owen Jarvis's granddaughters came to visit him saying, 'Granddad I have good news for you, but seeing that you do not know of it yet, I'll keep it a secret. But within three weeks' time you and Grandma will be going on a surprise mystery tour to the West Indies.' She would really have liked to be there to see her grandmother's face when she heard that she would be going to West Indies. She will be absolutely speechless because she has never visited the West Indies before.

Their granddaughter wouldn't be going with them. She would just wait and listen to their story when they returned to England again.

Three weeks later, Owen Jarvis and Deloris didn't really know how this happened, but it was dinner time when they found themselves at his parents' home in Jamaica. They were indeed lost for words, it being his wife's first visit to his parents' home, but she was very excited to be there.

Her husband and her mother-in-law took her for a walk around his parents' beautiful garden. There were a variety of things in the garden that she was allowed to take back to England with her. Her mother-in-law gave her the choice of anything that she wanted. She was sure excited, it being her first visit. Then, while in their excitement, suddenly a raven passed over the garden struggling to fly.

Deloris cried out, 'Owen Jarvis!' She pointed to the sky. Owen looked and saw a raven struggling to fly. 'Someone might have shot it,' his wife remarked. Then suddenly the raven landed onto the ground not far from where they were standing. 'Wow,' she cried out, frightened. 'Who would have shot the poor raven out of the sky?' she asked.

Owen Jarvis's mother said it has not been shot. 'My Revelation had come to pass before my very eyes. Not many days ago I had a Revelation that a time will come when all the ravens shall be devoured by the stoats.'

'Mum,' Owen Jarvis called out, frightened.

'How can that be?' Deloris said. 'The stoats cannot fly.'

'I know that,' she said, 'that's why it has lost its power and fell to the ground so that it can be eaten by the stoats.'

'Oh my God,' Owen cries out. They were all fearful that the end of the world might be at hand.

Owen Jarvis then thought of the scripture, Joel chapter 2 verse 1 and a sense of indignation began to fill him. That verse says, 'blow he the trumpet in Zion and sound an alarm in God's Holy mountain: let all the inhabitants of the land tremble for the day of the Lord cometh. It is near at hand'. The scripture says that day will be a day of darkness and of gloominess. A day of clouds and of thick darkness as the morning spread upon the mountains.

Then he thought that the raven that fell from the sky might be a warning to everybody that our Lord God and our Lord Jesus Christ might be coming back to earth soon. Then he thought of the scripture 1 Thessalonians chapter 4 verse 16 which said, 'For the Lord Himself shall descend from heaven with a shout, with the voice of the archangel, and with the trump of God: and the death in Christ shall rise first'. Verse 17 said, 'then those which are alive and remain shall be caught up together with them that rise up from the grave into the clouds to meet the Lord in the air, and so shall we forever be with the Lord'.

'Do you know why the Lord God is going to take His people out of this world?' Owen Jarvis asked his mum.

CHAPTER 51

THE RAVEN LOST ITS POWER

She spoke of Malachi, chapter 4 verse 1 that said, 'Behold the day of the Lord cometh, that shall burn as an oven and all the proud Yea and all that do wickedly, shall be stubble, and the day that cometh shall burnt them up sanity the Lord of host, it shall neither leave root nor branches'. Verse 2 said, 'But unto you that fear God's name shall the Sun of righteousness arise with healing in His wings'.

After they had heard those verses of the scripture, she said to them, 'We should all make sure that we are on the Lord's side before the day of His reappearance.' And they all agreed together and said amen. We should keep praying that our heavenly flight might not be in the winter months. They all said amen.

CHAPTER 52

THE COMMUNITY WORKERS

The young lady on the horse back is to remind us of those horse riders in the book of Revelations. Owen Jarvis's thoughts went back to the Revelation in which his mother had seen a raven suddenly lose its power to fly and fall out of the sky. Then that one night in 1977 he too had also had a vivid vision of God that caused he and his wife to become community workers. In his vision he saw many lawless children roaming the city being chased by police.

Ever since this man heard the voice of the Lord God, the excitement in his heart never went away. And so that he might justify his calling, not many days after he and his wife became community workers, so that the vision he had might become a reality.

CHAPTER 53

THE REVELATION OF GOD'S ARMIES

Revelation 9 V 1 to 15 and 16 told of the number of God's horsemen, two hundred thousand. K.J.V. After the great war then joy shall come in the morning. K.J.V. Revelation 21 I saw a new heaven and a new earth: for the first heaven and the first earth had passed away and there was no more sea. V2 said I John saw the holy city, the new Jerusalem coming down from God out of heaven prepared as a bride adorned for her husband.

This is just a hint. Please read the Revelation from the beginning, you will be surprised to know what is going to happen to all those who do not have God on their side.

This story is written so that you might return to your Lord and saviour before that day comes. God loves us so much He gave His son, Jesus Christ, so that all those who believe in him may live. And there all says, Amen. And this is. Amen to us all.

The End